THE PROMISE

RIVER LAURENT

AUTHOR'S NOTE

Hiya!

This book include an exclusive thank you for being my reader gift. He is one hot Alpha and can't wait to meet you!

Happy reading.

xoxo

ACKNOWLEDGMENTS

Contributors:
Brittany Urbaniak
Caryl Milton
Elizabeth Burns
Nicola Rhead

The Promise

ISBN: 978-1-911608-17-2

This book is dedicated to:
Georgia Le Carre
Thank you for being so amazingly generous and kind always!

COLE

S he fuckin' hates you, Cole Finley. Let it alone. You've survived all these years. Just damn well leave it alone.

But I can't.

Her smell is in my nostrils, which is plum stupid because while it's true she is back in town, she's miles away. Letty, who runs the Lake hotel, called to tell me that she arrived last night. From that moment on, I stopped being able to function.

Damnit to hell, but all I want to do is hold her warm curves again, feel her heart beating, fill my lungs with her breath.

My body feels as if it is an iron filing and a giant magnet is pulling at it. The draw is so strong I have to clench my hands into fists to stop from grabbing my car keys and going to her.

I glance at my watch for the hundredth time and pace the floor of my library restlessly. The funeral must surely be over by now.

A car comes up the driveway, and I stride over to the window. It's my mother. Impatiently, I watch her take her time getting out of her car and walk up to the door. She is still dressed in the black outfit she wore to the funeral. I turn away from the window, relax my hands, and wait while she travels through my house. I turn around and she is standing at the doorway.

"What does she look like?" I'd tried to keep my voice neutral, but it comes out hoarse and throbbing with need.

Her eyes widen with surprise.

I clench my jaw and stare at her. She better not even try to say anything.

She doesn't. With a defeated sigh, she heads to the drinks cabinet. Barely able to control myself, I wait while she pours out a large measure of vodka. No chaser. She drinks it down as if she needs it more than I do, and slams the glass down on the counter.

She turns towards me. "She looks like a star," she says flatly.

I run my hands through my hair. "But does she look happy?"

She raises her eyebrows. "She was attending her stepmother's funeral, so one shouldn't really expect cartwheels."

I glare at her with frustration, my shoulders tense. "You know what I mean. Does she look like she is happy with her life? Like she made the right decision to leave here?"

My mother shrugs delicately and walks over to a sofa. She settles herself and leans against the leather. "It's hard to say, but she looks like someone who no longer belongs in Black Rock."

My chest tightens with pain. Even breathing hurts. "Was she there … alone?"

Her eyes fill with pity. "Yes."

That one word feels like fireworks exploding inside my body. "Ma."

"Yes?"

"I need to see her again." My voice is clipped and hard.

My mother's face tightens. "Don't do that, Cole. She'll be gone by tomorrow and your life will go back to what it was. Don't spoil it. Don't make it harder for yourself … and her."

"I just want to see her for a moment."

She leans forward. Dr. Westwood's injections have made it impossible for her to frown, but I know that expression, she is trying to. "It's a terrible idea, Cole."

"I don't fucking care."

"Oh, darling. She'll destroy you."

I start backing away from her. "Then let her."

She gasps with horror.

"I just want to see how she is. After all this time, no one can begrudge me that one thing. If she's truly happy, I'll walk away. I swear it."

"Cole," my mother calls, but I am already at the front door.

I get into my car and hit the accelerator hard. The wheels spin on the asphalt. All those years ago she broke me, and maybe she will again, but I don't care. I have to see her one more time. There's been no one since she left. Every woman

3

leaves me cold. No matter what they do or say, I feel nothing. My cock is numb.

It is waiting for her.

TAYLOR

Alight spring breeze lifts the side-swept bangs off my forehead. The air smells clean with a hint of freshly dug earth. It makes a heavenly change from the smog of LA. I breathe it deeply into my lungs. Through the lenses of my dark glasses, I watch the priest say the last rites. His voice is gravelly and solemn, but I hardly hear the words.

"Ashes to ashes, dust to dust."

There should be sadness in my heart, instead there is nothing. I think of her as she was: beautiful and cold. No, cold is the wrong word. I guess she was bitter. She always viewed me as the competition, but when Dad died and left the house to me with the provision that she could live her life out in it, I became the enemy. How she hated me, silently, coldly, viciously.

While I lived with her I hated her back with an equal intensity, but after I left with a broken heart, I understood her bitterness. My father shouldn't have left the house to me. It was a betrayal. He should have left it to her. She was his wife.

I sent her money every month, which she neither acknowledged, or thanked me for.

I look down at my black Louboutins. I should have known better than to wear them. The heels are too high, and if I don't hold them with the spikes hovering slightly above the ground, they sink into the soft earth.

The priest stops speaking and turns his head to look at me, a questioning look in his eyes.

I drop the red rose in my hand on the glossy white casket and turn around to leave. People I have not seen or heard of/from for ten years mill around me. Their well-meaning faces filled with genuine kindness and regret. They are good people. I grew up with them. Almost family. I can't let them unravel me.

Smiling vaguely at no one in particular, I quickly start walking towards my car. Marco, my driver, rushes to open the door of the hired car. I slip in smoothly, and he closes the door with a click. I exhale. Relief floods my body. I've done my duty. I've given her a good burial.

Marco gets in and winds the partition down. "Hotel?"

"Yes," I confirm quietly.

"Right." He nods and activates the remote partition upwards.

"Wait," I blurt out.

The partition stops its upward journey.

"No. Not the hotel. Take me to my mother's house first."

"Got it," he says smartly.

The car travels through the main street of Black Rock, and it

6

is like being in a time warp. Nothing has changed, Dairy Queen, Tucker's Diner, the plastic dog outside the hardware shop. The green and white 'open' sign is still on the door of Chilli and Goose. Memories of my high school friends and I trying to buy beer crowd into my head.

There's old Jenkins, a beer can in his hand, sitting outside his tattoo shop sunning himself in the weak sunlight. His face is pure leather from the years he's spent in the sun, but he is still alive and well. We used to pop firecrackers into his mailbox and he would run out of his house, his face purple with rage, and screaming blue murder.

Marco drives up to the house.

The shutters are drawn. There is a sad air of stillness and neglect around it.

"You can go back to the hotel, Marco. I'll call you in the morning."

"You're sure?"

I nod and get out of the car. It is strange not to be mobbed by paparazzi and fans. Actually, it's rather wonderful not to have to run like a criminal from the car to the door all the time. For years, I believed I wanted fame. I wanted to be recognized everywhere I went. I wanted to be a big star, but now I know I don't.

Marco drives away and I go up the wooden steps to the wide porch. I glance at the rocking chair at one corner and feel an odd twinge. A feeling. How strange. I haven't felt anything for years. My cell rings, the sound muted, but oddly jarring. As if my other busy life has already come to intrude. I take it out of my purse and look at the screen. It's Nick, my manager. I walk to the rocking chair. Sitting in it I click accept.

"Where are you now?" he asks.

"At the house."

"You mean the funeral is already over?"

"Yeah," I reply distantly. I don't want to talk to him. The sound of the chair creaking against the wood is soothing. My mother used to sit here a lot with me in her lap after she fell ill. I close my eyes. Memories swarm back. Memories of Mom, memories of Dad, memories of Cole. My stomach clenches into a painful knot. I push the images away and open my eyes.

"Are you all right?" Nick sounds anxious, whether for me or my career is hard to tell, but he is definitely concerned. Probably for my career, I decide.

"Yes."

"You sure you don't want me to come?"

"Absolutely. I'm not hanging around long, anyway. I'll be leaving tomorrow afternoon."

"That's good. There's nothing left for you in that godforsaken town."

"No," I agree, but an ache deep inside me starts to throb. I left something here, Nick. I left my heart.

"All right, then. Call me if you need anything, or if you just want to talk, okay?"

"Okay."

"Love you," he says.

"Call you later."

I end the call, and try to think of Nick's warm brown eyes. He cares about me. He's a nice guy. We work well together. I have a good life in LA. I have a better than good life in LA. The past is just a mirage. There is nothing left here for me, but my eyes are drawn to the wise old, spreading magnolia tree.

The swing is gone, but my treehouse is still there, the rusty corrugated roof nearly completely hidden by leaves and overgrown ivy. The wind blows and I can hear the shutters squeaking on their hinges. Some of the planks of ladder are broken and it swings forlornly in the wind. I can still remember the smell of cheese in the mouse traps. Dad and I never caught any. They were too clever. Somehow, they had found a way to steal the cheese without triggering the cage door.

Once it was my secret hideaway.

A place where no one could see me.

No one could find me.

No one, but Cole.

TAYLOR

At six years of age

"Daddy, what if Mommy wakes up in the box and we've buried it?"

"She won't wake up, honey."

"How do you know?"

"Because she's gone. She's left her body and gone to heaven."

"Won't Mommy ever come back?" I ask, confused and worried.

"No, honey."

I look at Daddy curiously. "Why not? Doesn't she want to be with us?"

He makes a strange sound in his throat. It sounds like a sob. Then he takes a deep breath and smiles at me. "She does.

More than anything in the world she wanted to be with us, but God wanted her back. So she's an angel now. She lives in heaven."

"She does?"

He presses his lips together and nods.

I think about it. "Can we go and visit her?"

His throat moves.

"Can we, Daddy?"

"No, honey, we can't," he says finally, and hugs me so tight I can't even breathe.

"Daddy, you're choking me," I gasp.

He lets go of me instantly. "Sorry, honey."

"Daddy?"

"Yes." His voice is gentle.

"But I really, really miss Mommy."

"It is okay to miss Mommy, I'll miss Mommy too, a lot, but we shouldn't be sad she's gone, because she's in a better place. A much, much better place. Remember how much pain she was in?"

I think of her face, so white it was almost the color of the pillow case. "Yes."

"Well, she's not in pain anymore."

I nod slowly. "That's good. I didn't like it when Mommy was in pain."

"Neither did I," he says softly.

"Daddy. Can I write a letter to Mommy?"

"Yeah, you can write a letter to Mommy," he says with a heavy sigh. "But let's go downstairs first. All our friends are waiting for us."

When we go downstairs our house is full of people. They stare at me and give me funny looks while muttering and whispering together. I hear snatches of their conversation.

"She's just six years old. Poor mite."

"Wonderful woman."

"It's for the best. She was suffering, poor woman."

"So sad," the women whisper to Daddy. Men clap his back and tell him how sorry they are. People who I've never met try to hug me. I don't want to be hugged by them so I slip away and run out through the back door. I walk along the side of our house and climb up the magnolia tree. My hands and legs are so strong my father says I'm almost like a monkey.

Standing against the back wall of my treehouse, I slide down to the floor and extend my legs to their full length. My white tights are clean and smudge free and my knee-length dress with its velvet bow makes me feel like a princess, but my shoes are hot and they squish my feet. Daddy made me wear them because they are Mommy's favorite, but what's the point if she's gone to heaven and will never be coming back.

Actually, I've already started to miss her a lot.

From the corner of my eyes I can see my Barbie sitting on the floor where I left her two days ago. It's been many days since I changed her clothes or combed her hair. She won't like it. We both have the same hair color but hers is long and mine is shorter. I reach for my Princess crown and put it on my head. Now my outfit is complete. I turn my head and look at the mirror on the wall that Daddy hung up for me.

My face looks white. I don't know why, but it feels as if something inside me is broken. I think I just want Mommy to come back. I'm very worried about her ever since I saw her sleeping in the box. I don't understand how she will get to heaven from inside the box. Will she be all alone? I hope Daddy is wrong. I hope she comes back soon. Tears gather in my eyes and roll down my face. I sniff and wipe them away with the backs of my hands. I want to be brave just in case Mommy is watching from heaven.

"Hi," I hear from the entrance of my treehouse.

I whip my head around half in fear and half in shock, and spring to my feet, my shiny black shoes clanking on the floor. The intruder has popped his head inside my doorway. Nobody ever comes up here, let alone a dark-haired, hazel-eyed boy! "You can't come in here. Boys aren't allowed," I yell.

"I'm sorry about your mom," he says calmly.

"You don't have to be sorry. My mom is in a better place. She's an angel now," I explain. I don't expect him to understand. His mommy is probably still on earth.

"Can I come in?" he asks.

I crinkle my nose and squint my eyes at him. Boys have cooties, but he looks pretty clean...

"I brought you a flower," he says softly.

He brought me a flower, so he might not have cooties. "All right. Just for a minute."

He pulls himself into the treehouse, bringing the flower into view. "I saw you come up here. My mom said girls like flowers when they're sad."

"I'm not sad," I hiss, sitting back on the floor.

I watch him fill the doorway, then take a few steps forward. "Sometimes you don't have to cry to be sad," he says, sitting beside me. He stretches his legs out the same as me. His are much longer than mine.

I take the daisy from him. The flower is as big as my hand. "What's your name?"

"Cole," he says.

"I'm Taylor Rose."

"I know. Your dad works for my dad," he explains. "I live in the big house at the top of the hill."

Everyone knows about the house at the top of the hill. The most famous family in town lives in the house.

"Are you famous too?"

Cole turns his face towards me. He has very long eyelashes for a boy. "I'm not famous. I think we're just rich. At least, I've heard people say that we're rich."

"Oh," I say, disappointed. I stare into the face of the flower. I don't know what it means to be rich, but it would be cool if Cole were famous. I want to be famous. I've always wanted to be famous. My bedroom is filled with posters of Brittany Spears and other famous celebrities.

"Do you like the flower?" he asks me with a broad smile. Cole is cute and I want to be his friend.

"It's really pretty. Thank you."

"How come I don't see you at school?"

"I don't know. I'm in first grade."

He grins. "I'm not."

"You play with nerf guns?" Cole asks, looking at my stack of nerf guns. "I thought little girls played with dolls and stuff."

"I like baby dolls, but Nerf guns are fun. I have a target too, see?" I say, walking to the side of the room and hanging it on the wall.

I don't think about mommy as we play with the Nerf guns. I'm good at shooting, so I almost beat Cole, but he's better. We continue to talk until his parents yell for him. He says goodbye. After he leaves I hold the flower in my hands and smell it. It has no scent. I never had a favorite flower before, but I think daisies are my favorite flower now.

TAYLOR

Present Day

I shake myself out of my daydream. That was another lifetime. Nothing remains of that world. Suddenly, I am filled with curiosity to know what the inside of my treehouse looks like now. Probably the home of squirrels or something.

Later I will go and explore it.

I slip my shoes off, take the key from under the flower pot, and open the front door. Inside it is dim and full of still blue shadows.

I close the door quietly, lean against it and breathe in the air. It smells stale and musty, with a strong chemical odor of medicine underneath it. My step-mother lived here alone for the last eight years. For the final two she was very sick. I let my eyes move around the quiet space. This is now mine. Well, it was always mine, but all I can feel is her deep resentment as if she is still alive, and sitting in behind the closed door of the living room.

Coming back was a mistake.

There is nothing here for me.

For a moment, I have an overwhelming desire to walk out of the house and get Marco to come fetch me, but I can't bear the thought of all those well-meaning people at the hotel. I don't want to wear my pop star being gracious to her fans mask. I feel so tired I just need to sleep for a few hours.

The doorbell rings and the sound startles me. I look through the peephole and see Mrs. Tucker from next door standing outside. She is in her Sunday best. Suppressing a sigh, I school my features into one of polite enquiry and open the door.

"Hello, Taylor," she beams. "I've brought you some casserole. I thought we could have lunch together."

I don't know where she got the idea of having lunch with me. I can't remember an occasion when we had lunch together. I hang onto the doorknob and plaster a smile on my face. "Thank you, Mrs. Tucker. That is so kind of you, but honestly, I'm just not in the mood to eat anything right now."

Her face falls which kinda makes me feel guilty, but I just can't face having to make small talk with anyone right now. She holds the container out to me. "Well then, honey, you eat it when you feel hungry. I'll be next door if you need me."

Reluctantly, I take the casserole I know I will never eat. "Thank you."

She turns to go then pauses, before spinning back with

remarkable agility. "I've followed your career, you know. You've done our little town proud, my girl. Both Mr. Tucker and I are very proud of you."

"Thank you, Mrs. Tucker," I say politely.

"Well, I just thought you should know."

"It's very kind of you to say that. Thank you." I smile again.

"Well, all right. I'll be going, then."

"Good bye, Mrs. Tucker."

I put the casserole on the kitchen table, and the doorbell goes again. With a frown, I go to answer it. It'll probably be another neighbor bearing more food I can't eat. I don't even bother to look through the peephole this time. I open the door to Betty Crankshaw. She is wearing a blue hat and carrying a cake tin.

"There you are, dear. I knew you must be feeling terrible so I've brought some blueberry muffins for you. I know how much you love my muffins."

Muffins are off the menu for me, but I smile broadly at her. "That's very kind of you, Mrs. Crankshaw. Thank you."

COLE

I speed through a red traffic light and turn into Mullholland drive. I've not been here since she left. I park the car outside her mother's house and get out, my heart thudding so hard I can hear it. Betty Crankshaw is turning out of her gate.

She stops and nods at me.

"Mrs. Crankshaw," I greet with a nod.

"That girl is as skinny as a rake, Cole," she mutters, tutting disapprovingly.

She obviously wants to stand there and talk to me, but I make a gesture with my hand to indicate that I'm in a hurry, and hurry past her. I stride up to the door and ring the bell. It goes unanswered for such a long time and I'm about to ring it again when she opens the door.

The moment I see her face I regret ever letting her go. My heart aches with need. God, how stupid I was. What a fucking kid I must have been to let her go.

And for what?

Look at her.

She's not happy.

She used to glow with happiness. I should have chained her to me instead of letting her go to carve her name in lights. It was a mistake. I have to make her fall back in love with me again.

Her full lips part. "Cole," she breathes, and for a second it is as if no time has passed. The other kids are singing Cole and Taylor K-i-s-s-i-n-g in the Tree to us. She's my girl and I've come around to take her to the movies. I stare at her mouth. I'm dying for a taste. She used to taste of honey.

Then the past disappears like smoke, and her eyes become hard. "What do you want, Finley?"

"You," the word flies out of my mouth.

Something flashes in her eyes. "You're a bastard, you know?"

"I should never have let you go, Taylor."

"Get out of my house," she growls, her eyes stormy.

"I'm not leaving without you."

"What? she sneers. "Has alcohol addled your brain? Because we were finished eight years ago."

Inwardly, I wince at the jibe, but I look her straight in the eye. "We're not finished until I say so."

She moves suddenly to slam the door, but I put my palm out, completely arresting its movement.

"Do I need to call the police?" she huffs.

"All I want to do is talk to you."

"There's nothing to talk about." Her voice is bitter.

"Then it'll be a very short conversation, won't it?"

For a few seconds our gazes clash, then she sighs, an oddly defeated sound, and moves away from the door.

"Say what you need to say and get out," she throws over her shoulder as she leads the way into her mother's sitting room.

I go into the house and close the door.

"Talk," she says, turning to face me and folding her arms in front of her stiff body.

"Did you achieve everything you wanted? Was it worth it?"

"Yes," she snarls, her voice trembling defiantly.

I start walking towards her.

Her eyes fill with panic, and she takes an instinctive step backwards. "I'm glad I grabbed the opportunity when it presented itself and left this god-forsaken town."

I stare down at her glittering eyes. "No regrets?"

"None." The word is smooth and hard, penetrating like a bullet.

I look at her face and know I cannot go another day, hour, or minute without making her mine. "Well, I have. I should have done it differently. I want you, Taylor. I've been wanting you for the last eight years. I've waited all this time, but no more. I won't be denied for another second. I'm going to have you right now."

Her eyes widen. She shakes her head. "No," she gasps, but I

notice she doesn't move away. I move in for the kill. Wrapping my hands around her too thin body, I let my mouth descend down on hers, crushing, hungry, fierce.

She whimpers with the force of my kiss.

I lean in and lift her up into my arms. Her hands go around my neck. Her round eyes stare up at me, helpless, vulnerable … mine. I lift her into my arms. Fuck, it's like picking up a child. Doesn't she ever eat anything in LA?

I carry her up those old stairs. We are not in our twenties. We are teenagers again. Her stepmother has gone to play bridge and I have slipped in through the window. She has abandoned the bowl of ice cream she was eating. I am taking her upstairs again.

She burrows her face in my chest, but I can feel her trembling like a frightened bird in my arms. I hear her shallow breaths. The stairs creak under our weight. I kick the door open to her old room. Her stepmother has kept it almost exactly how it was when she was living there.

I lay her on the single bed and look down at her. The bedspread is covered in blue roses. A long time ago I made her mine on this bed.

She is about to find out nothing has changed. She belongs to me and only me.

COLE

10 YEARS OLD

I don't know how to approach the situation, but I know she needs me. I make my way up the old, weathered tree-house ladder. When I reach the entrance, Taylor is sitting in a corner, face hidden between her knees.

Her long blonde hair flows over her arms and brushes the floor. It envelopes her entire body and makes her look smaller than usual, and she's already a petite girl. The sight of her makes my chest ache. If I could I would take her pain.

"Taylor," I whisper.

She looks up, and when we make eye contact, I am shocked.

I've never seen her cry. When her mother died, she didn't cry. When she finally realized that her mother was really never coming back, she was heartbroken, but she didn't cry. When her dad remarried within a year, she didn't cry. Taylor has never allowed herself to cry in front of me.

Until now.

Her eyes are red and raw and her shoulders shake as great sobs are torn out of her mouth.

"Go away," she cries. Even her voice is tearful and raw.

I stay frozen, still shocked by her appearance. We've been best friends for four years, but I've never seen her this way.

"Please, Cole. I don't want you to see me cry," she begs hoarsely.

"Why not?" I whisper.

Her lower lip trembles and she presses her hand on her mouth. "You don't need to see me crying."

"Taylor, I don't care if you cry. If my dad died, I would cry too," I say gently, taking a hesitant step in her direction. At the mention of father, her tears flow more freely and her shoulders heave even more rapidly.

Not knowing what to say, I kneel silently in front of her. I felt sorry for her when her mom died and she was left with only one parent, but now her father is gone as well. She has nobody left. She is an orphan. I can't even imagine how she must be feeling.

"Just go away and I'll be fine tomorrow," she pleads.

I frown. "I'm your friend and friends see each other cry. They help each other when the going gets rough."

She sniffs. "But Cassie said she heard from the other boys that the only reason you are friends with me is because I'm tough and I don't act like a girl."

"I don't know where Cassie got her information from, but that's just not right. I'm friends with you because you're tough. And I'm friends with you because you don't act like a girl. But I'm also your best friend because you're funny and fun. And we dig the same foods and go to the same school and you have a cool treehouse where we do our homework." I sit down next to her as her crying comes to a halt. She's no longer bawling and I'm relieved.

"So you'll still be my friend after this?" she asks.

"I'll always be your friend." I grab a hold of her hand and she squeezes it. Then she lays her head on my lap. I stare down at her blonde head in astonishment. Very slowly my hand lifts up and I lay it on her head. Her hair is silky. Awkwardly, I start to stroke her soft hair. Almost hypnotized, I watch my hand as it smooths the tangled gold strands.

"I'm all alone, Cole. What's going to happen to me now?" Taylor asks with a sniffle.

I shake my head. "I don't know, but you'll always have me."

"Promise?"

She turns her head and looks up at me. I stare into her wet eyes and I feel as fierce as a tiger. "I promise. No matter what happens around us I will always be there for you. I will take care of you and never let anything bad happen to you until the day I die."

COLE

PRESENT DAY

She looks up at me, her eyes enormous, and licks her lips. "Do you have a ... condom?"

I shake my head slowly. She doesn't understand. She really doesn't get it. "There has never been anything to come between us, not even a thin film of rubber, and there never will be."

I see her throat muscles work when she swallows hard. "That's all right, I'm on the pill, anyway."

It hurts me to hear that. I've seen those other men being mentioned in the press. I blank out the thought. It is beneath me. Unworthy. I don't give a shit about the other men. They don't count. How can they? They were the gum she chewed without satisfaction and discarded quickly.

The past doesn't exist. It is only me and her. It has always been only me and her. A thousand men can enter her body, and it wouldn't change a thing. She will always be mine. Bound forever. Body, mind, and soul.

I run my finger along her plump bottom lip making her shiver. "You're not going to fight me, are you?"

She closes her eyes, takes a deep breath, then shakes her head.

I reach for a glossy button on her little black jacket. Her body sways towards me. The round buttons slip out of their eyelets easily revealing the expensive silky dress underneath. I've never liked her in black and yet I keep seeing her in it. Something about the severity of the style grates on my nerves. I hook my fingers into the modest V neckline and tear it clean down the middle.

She gasps with shock.

Yes, Taylor, I was a boy then. I am a man now. A man who is taking what's his. She lies on the single bed in her lacy, half-cup white bra and panties. All in white. That surprises me. I look into her eyes.

"What?" she whispers.

My nerve endings fire erratically. The intensity of my desire to pounce on her makes me sweat. Hell, my dick feels like a piece of fucking wood digging into my stomach. I touch her stomach and her warm skin trembles. "Why did you wear white?"

She shrugs coolly, but her eyes slip away from mine. "No reason."

"Liar," I mock softly.

Color spreads up her neck and cheeks, and memories come crashing back. Of the first time I took her. Stripping her slowly. The cheap green blouse. The ripped blue jeans.

Until she lay in her virginal cotton underwear. I remember confessing I can never resist her in white. Her giggling. 'So I should always wear white underwear when I want to seduce you?' Me not giggling, and replying. 'Without exception.'

I feel my body vibrating with the intensity of my desire.

The bra has a front opening. I unclasp it and free her breasts. They are smaller than I remember. All of her is smaller than I remember. I kneel down and take a pink nipple in my mouth. She gasps, her body arching, her silken thighs falling open.

Through her panties, I savor her heady scent and lick her swollen clit.

"Cole," she cries.

I kiss and lap at her clothed crotch.

Her hands are clawing at the bedspread. "Take it off," she says, panting and squirming.

"Tell me how bad you want me to eat you."

"Don't make me beg, Cole," she whines, turning her head from side to side.

Goddamn, but she's going to beg for it. I lick her pussy again, wetting the blonde curls.

"Oh, yessss," she hisses, jerking her hips with frustration.

"Tell me you want my hot tongue deep inside you, Taylor."

She is too lust induced to deny me, or even care what she is saying anymore. Grinding, rubbing, and gyrating her hips restlessly against my mouth, she blindly gasps out, "Yes, please … please, get your tongue inside me. Like before.

Deep inside. Eat me out, Cole ... eat me out because I need it. It's been so ... so long."

Her body belongs to me. I have always been able to make it do exactly what I want. I pull to one side the scrap of lace between us. Underneath her pussy is as pink as a rose. Parting the soft folds, I expose her dripping entrance. I thought I was in control, but the sight of her throbbing core drives me wild.

In one smooth movement my tongue dives deep into her eager pussy. She's right: it's been so damn long. She has no idea what it means to me to be back inside her again. To enjoy the taste and smell of her. All those painful years of terrible longing fall away as I lap at her nectar, savoring every sweet lick, devouring her.

"Oh, Cole," she moans again and again.

I feel her thighs begin to quiver and her body arch. She is almost there. I push two fingers inside her. Sweet Jesus! She feels exactly the same. As tight as the first time I slipped a tentative finger into her virgin pussy. I find her g-spot and apply pressure to it while I suck her clit into my mouth.

"Cole," she groans, as she pushes her throbbing pussy against my flicking tongue.

I feel her body climbing towards her peak. "Cum for me, Taylor. Let me see you break apart."

Instantly, her back becomes a bow, her legs lock around my head, and her mouth opens in a soundless scream. As wave after wave of pleasure hits her, warm liquid gushes out of her and runs down my mouth and chin. I've missed her taste. There is no other woman in the world who tastes like my

Taylor. It is a deliciously long climax and I drink down her juices eagerly.

Once her orgasm is entirely wrung out, and her body stops bucking, she touches one side of my face with her fingertips. So gently I can barely feel them as they trace my face, from my jaw up to my cheek.

Her expression takes my breath away. I want to believe it. I know it is truth. This is how she truly feels. Everything else is just bullshit. The fame, the money, the adulation, that's not real.

I rip away the soaking wet lace before standing to gaze down at her, naked, sated, limp. Her legs are open and her pussy is swollen and still throbbing. I've been thinking about her this way as I stroked myself to release for years. I want Taylor's naked body with every fiber of my being. I've always wanted her this way. Never at any time, has there been another woman for me.

Only her.

Her eyes burn into mine and her face has an erotic glow to it. She knows what's coming and she's as horny as a woman can get. I unzip my jeans and her eyes drop to my hands.

I smile. "Open up for me, Taylor. Give me a show. Like you used to."

As I remove my clothes, never taking my eyes off her, she fondles herself while lifting her legs high and straight into the air, then she spreads them wide apart to show me her open pussy.

"Rub your own clit."

She brings two fingers to her mouth and sucks them in. Memories come flooding back. Fuck, we had it so good and we never even knew. We were so stupid. She brings those wet fingers to her swollen pussy and starts stroking herself. Her thighs are strong from all the grueling tours and stage performances she does, and she keeps the V straight and strong as I position myself between her thighs.

"Hell, Taylor, I'm going to ride you so hard."

Grabbing my cock, I rub the tip in her wetness before moving to her entrance still glistening with her juices and my saliva. As her pussy clenches tightly around the head of my raw cock, I thrust fully into her, all the fucking way. She cries out, and I lean down and swallow her cry with my mouth. Her lips soften as my tongue sweeps inside her mouth, tasting her.

I lift my head. "Relax. It's just me, baby. You love my cock, remember?"

"Yes, but go slow."

"I'll go as fast as I want and you'll take it. Ya' hear me."

"Yes," she grunts breathlessly.

"Good, because I remember that your cunt is a greedy little thing and I intend to fill her with my cock all night."

At my forceful words her pussy squeezes and gushes onto my cock. Nothing has changed. Dirty talk still turns my Taylor on. I start to move in and out, my thrusts quick and shallow, until I feel her body begin to melt and open up for me.

"That's my girl. Now fuck me back."

I pull almost completely out of her and slam back in. A loud moan escapes her lips, but her body responds, her hips rise up to meet my plunges. She starts to match my speed as I go faster and faster. Her pussy grips my cock as strongly as a fist every time I withdraw out of her.

"Fuck you feel so good. I'm going to fill you with my cum."

"Yes," she whispers. "Yes, I want it."

We go at it until we are one sweaty, rutting pile of flesh. I feel her body curve and her throat stretch out as she gets close to her climax. It is an invitation. I lean in and bite her neck. That is all it takes. She screams out my name as she falls over the edge. I follow her, my cock pulsing streams of hot seed into her body.

TAYLOR

I come awake, but don't open my eyes right away. If I do and find out I'm alone, it would all have been a dream. Some part of me believes what happened earlier doesn't really happen in real life. No one is that lucky. That kind of intensity is just in the movies, or in the pages of romance novels.

Call me cynical, but show business gives you a front row view of the ugly underbelly of human interactions. Just one layer beneath the shiny façade of the air-brushed, impossibly beautiful celebrity are bloody fangs and talons. I'm not a kid anymore. I've been around the block enough times to know there are no magical happy endings. Everybody is out for themselves. They can pretend to be your friend, but put them in a position of them or you and you soon see you have no friends. Cole is no friend of mine.

Yet, it must have happened, because my body's sore in that old 'I just had sex with big ole Cole' kind of way. The sort of sore that's nothing to do with hours of getting my butt kicked by my personal trainer. A delicious sore, the sort of sore I could do with every day of my life.

Judging from the sound of soft, rhythmic breathing behind me and warmth radiating from his body onto my naked skin, he's still here with me too.

I guess I always knew if I came back that I would sleep with him. I just thought I would have been able to resist him a bit longer. Not tumble like a house of cards at the first shot.

I blame his eyes. Ugh, those eyes. Gold-flecked hazel, familiar, beautiful, and completely hypnotic. One look into them and I actually felt years of resolve melt away. I've never seen eyes like his on anybody else. And those eyes looked into mine when our bodies melded, when he was on me, and in me. Making me whisper his name.

Cole. Oh, Cole.

Again and again. As if it was some kind of holy chant.

That was a moment of weakness, but now that the passion has passed there is nothing left. Nothing other than lost lust. I can't forgive him for the past, hell I don't want to. If there's one thing I know, it's that. I won't be anybody's doormat no matter how much I crave their body.

I suddenly remember the smell of the alcohol on his breath. God, was he even sober when he showed up at the house? My mind engages with that thought and I spiral into self-doubt. Oh, my God! Did I just let Cole Finlay use me to slake his lust? Then another voice, wiser, cuts in. No way was he drunk. A drunk man couldn't perform the way he did.

He was stone cold sober.

I open my eyes, and it is dark outside. Moonlight spills in through the windows. I squint at the clock on the wall. It is nearly ten, which means I've been asleep for hours. I must have been more tired than I thought.

What do I do now?

My insides tighten with a mixture of anxiety and excitement. The smart thing would be to slip out quietly and go straight to the hotel. Never see him again. Having an awkward post-mortem with Cole would be too much to deal with in my vulnerable state of mind. It would make everything I felt earlier seem ... like a mistake. It was not a mistake. I'm not ashamed of my desire. I wanted him and I let myself take what I wanted.

Now it is time to be strong, and walk away.

The thought of leaving like a thief in the night fills my being with an old sadness. My heart starts aching for him. No matter how much I pretend to myself, the truth is always there, glaring at me.

That I have never found any man, no matter how good-looking or rich, who can hold a candle to Cole. I cannot replace him because he remains the only one I let into my heart and who then proceeded to break it. They say the first cut is the deepest and it's true. He was my first love, the man I trusted, adored, and would have done anything for.

Not wanting to wake him up, I turn very slowly to look at him, and freeze.

His eyes are open, alert, and watching.

The sight makes my mind go utterly blank. Crap, crap, double crap. Needing to say something, anything, I open my mouth. Before I can articulate a single sound he lays a finger on my lips.

"Don't."

I stare at him wordlessly. Those hypnotic eyes suck me in, robbing me of speech, thought. His arms slide around me, pulling me to him. Oh, God, it feels so good—not just physically. My heart feels good. My soul. Something slips into place with an almost audible *Click!* when our bodies touch, his front to my back.

"Since you're booked to stay for two days at the hotel," he murmurs in my ear.

My mouth forms the word 'how'.

He looks amused. "Have you forgotten, Taylor? This isn't LA. Everyone knows everyone's business. As I was saying, since you're down here anyway, unless you plan to get very bored, you should spend the next two days with me."

I frown. This, I did not expect. Does he expect us to just carry on where we left off before? "Are you crazy? I can't forget, or forgive what you did, Cole."

His jaw hardens. "Don't forgive or forget if you find it impossible, but you owe me these two days, Taylor."

I feel a surge of fury run through my body. "Owe you?" I explode. "After what you did? How dare you?"

I try to jump out of the bed, but he grabs my shoulders and holds me tight. His expression doesn't change. "I dare, because it is the truth. Just because I did one thing wrong, one mistake, it doesn't cancel out everything else. Who took care of you for all those years? I put you before me. Every fucking time."

The anger leaves me as suddenly as it came. Cole is not lying. I do owe him. Big time. He protected and looked out for me. I don't even know how I would have survived my childhood without him. I take a deep shuddering breath. "You hurt me, Cole."

A cloud passes his face. "I know and I'm very sorry. I wish it hadn't happened that way, but it did, and there's not a damn thing I can do about it now. Perhaps I never will be able to take away that hurt, but I damn well want to try to make it up to you."

"I can't trust you, Cole. When I really needed you, you let me down."

"I'm not asking for your trust. I just want to spend two days with you."

"What happens after the two days?"

"If you don't want anything more, then nothing. You can go back to LA and resume your life. I won't stop you."

I hesitate. "I don't know, Cole. Sometimes it is best to let sleeping dogs lie. Like you said we have both changed."

"Exactly. Isn't it time we put the past behind us? We were kids then, Taylor. Two kids who didn't know better. We're adults now, and lots of things have changed, but one thing hasn't: we're both crazy about each other's bodies. Why can't we just have two days of mindless sex, then part as friends?"

I bite my lip and consider his words. God, his offer is so

tempting. I was only half alive without him. All these years I could never stop thinking of what might have been, never stop being angry with him for forcing me to break our relationship.

I can't go through the rest of my life hating him for something that happened so many years ago. We're both mature now and it is very likely we'll find that we are strangers who cannot get on anymore. Maybe these feelings I have for him have no basis in reality. All those warm memories are just a mirage. Yes, maybe it is a good idea. Then, I can leave this town and the past behind.

"You have nothing to lose," he says persuasively.

"So this will just be a physical thing."

"It'll be whatever you want it to be."

"I want it to be purely physical," I confirm quickly, even though my heart hurts a little when I say it. It is not at all what I want it to be.

"So be it. We will spend the next two days together then you will return to your life in LA."

"And you will return to yours."

"I will return to mine," he echoes softly, and bending his head, takes my nipple in his mouth. Instantly, my body arches up towards him.

TAYLOR

11 YEARS OLD

"She hates me," I say, loading a foam bullet into the Nerf gun and shooting Cole in the back of the head.

"Damn it, Taylor. Quit shooting me with that thing," he shouts, throwing the bullet back at me.

With little regard for his tone or words, I do the same thing again. He stands with his shoulders slouched and his neck bent. The treehouse isn't made for a six-foot fourteen-year-old boy. He comes over to me and snatches the gun from my hands and walks away to go sit against the other wall.

"She hates me," I repeat.

"She doesn't hate you. You're a teenager—well, almost—and she doesn't know how to deal with you," he retorts, throwing a green ball against the wall I am leaning on. It bounces smoothly back into his hand. I wonder how much longer this treehouse will remain standing. It wasn't built to be completely weather proof, and the floor and walls are starting to rot, but somehow still holding together.

"The only reason she hasn't put me on the street is because Dad's will made her my custodian and left a stipulation that if she kicks me out she loses the house. And she does hate me," I insist.

"Saying that she hates you is a little overboard, don't you think? She's your stepmother and she hasn't exactly done you any harm."

I raise an eyebrow and throw my last Nerf bullet in his direction to get his attention.

He looks at me angrily.

I scowl back. "This morning she told me that her life would be easier if I would have died along with dad."

"Wait, she said that?" Cole asks, turning his undivided attention to me.

I sigh and reach for the basket of knick-knacks. There aren't many things inside the treehouse anymore. We discarded most of the toys and breakables when we realized that it may fall soon. The Nerf gun and bullets didn't get thrown away for sentimental reasons.

"She can't even stand to look at me because Dad left the house to me. She says I'm ungrateful, but what have I got to be grateful for? She hardly cooks and her cooking sucks anyway. I clean my own room. We live off Dad's pension. Why did Dad have to die and leave me here? Sometimes I wish I could just have gone into foster care."

He frowns. "Don't say that. If you had gone into foster care we wouldn't be friends anymore. We'd never see each other."

"Actually, I've been thinking," I begin, twirling my hair with a small smile.

"What do you want me to do?" he asks with a groan.

"None of this would matter if we were famous."

"We're not."

"We could be. I know you are unbelievable at playing the guitar and I can sing and we can be a team. We'll have to find a catchy name for us and everything," I say excitedly.

"You sing and I play the guitar?" he repeats half-heartedly.

"Okay, I know you aren't into the idea of being a musician because you're convinced it will ruin your reputation, but I swear I won't say a word to anybody. We could practice in secret in the basement."

He looks at me doubtfully.

"I'm going to make something of myself, but I want you to be with me when I go big. I don't want to leave you behind," I negotiate.

"You want us to become rich and famous together?"

"That's exactly what I want. We'll be a team forever and ever."

He sighs and runs his hands through his hair. Cole leans forward and places both of his elbows on his knees and looks at me intently. "If I do this, will I get to see you every day?"

I nod rapidly. "Totally. We'll have to practice every day for hours and hours though."

"And if I don't become part of your team, how often will I see you?"

I shrug. "Maybe once a week, but sometimes we may go a week or even two without seeing each other. It depends on what I end up doing."

"So you're determined to become rich and famous?"

"That's the goal. I won't stop until I become famous," I say decisively.

"Then I'll do it. We'll become rich and famous together."

We bump knuckles in agreement and I smile at Cole. I won't be alone on my journey. I'll have my best friend at my side.

"Mmm … I'm starving," Cole murmurs.

"Starving for what?" I can't help wriggling against him a little, and what I feel growing against my lower back makes me smile. "Food or something else?"

"Is both a good answer?"

"Both is acceptable," I whisper and his arms tighten around me. He squeezes a little too hard, but I don't care. I wouldn't tell him to let go for anything in the world. I wish we could hide out in this room forever. The world outside be damned.

"There's lasagna in the fridge. I could warm it up for you," I offer, even though it's been a long time since I've been anywhere near a stove.

His brow furrows. "You hate lasagna."

"That's true, but I won't be eating it. You will."

"When was the last time you ate?"

"Breakfast."

"I know. Half a grapefruit." He grins at my surprised face. "The gossip mill works better than you think."

"Hmmm … yes, that. Mrs. Crankshaw brought blueberry muffins earlier. Want that?"

"Nah, I need real food. The last time I ate was last night."

My eyes widen. "How come?"

"Guess?" he says dryly and looks at his watch. "It's only eleven. Want to go out for something to eat?"

"Are there any places still open at this time of the night?" I ask with a smile.

"Uh, yeah. Black Rock didn't turn into a ghost town after you left."

I elbow him in the ribs. "Very cute." He jerks away with a chuckle. For a moment we are old friends again. Then my smile dies when I imagine seeing people—or, rather, letting them see me. Do I feel like dealing with that?

"What's the matter? You went away just then."

He always could read my subtle shifts in mood. "It's nothing. Where do you wanna go?"

"I thought maybe we could check out Artie's."

"What?" I sit up, eyes wide and grinning. "You seriously want to go down Memory Lane tonight, huh?"

His eyes drop down to my breasts. "Why the hell not? We're already more than halfway down the road. Might as well keep going, right?"

"Oi you. Can you concentrate? Eyes up here, please."

He brings his eyes up to my face, and his smile lights up the room, a smile I could never say no to. Gosh, to have his confidence. He knows he'll get his way, just like always. "The view is very distracting, but yeah, I want to go down memory lane with you."

"Okay. You're asking for it."

"What's that mean?"

I don't answer—my cryptic smile is all he gets before I get out of bed and buck naked walk to open my old wardrobe. I turn back and find him watching me. He doesn't smile. He's about to get an idea of what fame is like. I hope he can handle it.

***

The second we walk into the bar, all heads turn in our direction—or, rather, mine.

"Oh, my God! It's her!" I hear excited whispers and a few high-pitched squeals as we look around for a place to sit.

The bar is packed, as it always was in the days when Cole and I performed here. It's unthinkable, all these years later, that two kids in their mid-teens performed together at a bar full of drinkers who got steadily louder with each drink and smoked like it was their jobs. We thought we were so grown up back then. So sophisticated because we played gigs in a bar.

"Is it always like this?" Cole asks as we sit at a corner table. Even away from most of the crowd, the weight of the stares following my every movement is heavy. There are phones popping out everywhere, taking pictures and snagging video. What does Taylor order when she's out and about? What's her drink of choice? Who's the guy she's with—a new boy toy? Oh, I can hear the speculation circling around in my head already, and we haven't even seen a waitress yet.

"This is tame," I say with a shrug.

"You mean it gets crazier than this?" he asks with a laugh.

I raise an eyebrow. "Too much for you?"

"Not at all. I love watching my ex stir up a mob scene."

My smile wobbles just a little bit. There he said it. That's all we are. I wish I had the nerve to challenge him on it, but I'm too cowardly. "Famous last words," I joke instead. *Don't ruin this. This is how I want it. We're having fun. I have another life outside this town, away from him.*

The waitress looks like she just got out of high school—and like she might've fought her coworkers for the chance to serve our table. "Hi, my name is Emma and I'll be serving you tonight. You're Taylor Rose, aren't you?" she gushes. "I mean, I figure it's you since it looks like you and since everybody knows you're from around here and my friends heard you were in town, but we never thought you would come in here, like, ever."

I don't think she took a breath once during that whole speech. I give her my standard smile. She's just a star-struck small town kid. Once I was her. "Yup, that's me. Home for family stuff and starving half to death."

She giggles breathlessly. "Wow. That's amazing."

We could be here all night. I pick up one of the menus she

put on the table. "Can I have a Perrier with a twist of lemon, no ice."

She nods vigorously, before turning to Cole for the first time since she approached the table. I watch him curiously. He's not used to playing second fiddle when it comes to women. He's used to girls falling over him, offering to have his babies, or detail his car or whatever he wants just because he walks into a room.

"Oh, hi!" She flips her hair. I was wrong. The Cole Finlay effect is just as strong as ever. Apparently, no hormone producing female can resist him. "So, what can I get you?"

"You have any lager on tap?"

Emma thrusts her breasts forward in an unconsciously flirtatious way. "Sure. Seasonal okay?"

"Yeah. And a bacon burger, medium."

She turns to me. "Have you decided what you'd like?"

I was going to order the grilled chicken without Arties famous sauce smothered all over it, but Cole speaks.

"She'll have the same as me and bring her a lager too."

I should be angry at his high-handed behavior, but what the hell? When in Rome, order as the Romans do. Besides, I'm sick of organic this and vegan that. I'm craving some grease, and one of Artie's thick homemade juicy burgers will do the trick nicely. I can restart my diet when I get back to LA. I hand the menu back to Emma with a shrug.

"And an order of fries, too, please!" I call out as she leaves. A glance around reveals that I'm still the center of attention and my every word is up for dissection. Tomorrow some blog will be discussing how Taylor ordered fries after eleven at night.

"That kid was in danger of passing out," Cole notes when Emma is out of earshot.

"Yeah, the younger ones can get really intense."

He nods slowly. "And you like it?"

I shrug. "I was like that too. Remember?"

"Yeah. I remember." There is a weird tense moment, then Cole deliberately changes tack. "Remember all the times we spent here?" he asks, looking around.

"How could I forget?" I point to the stage, still sitting in one corner of the room. It's empty at the moment. A little sad. Or maybe it's me that's sad. No, I'm not sad I'm just feeling nostalgic for something lost. I'm experiencing a kind of bittersweet moment. We might've been performing for peanuts, but we were happy. No doubt about that.

Our beers arrive, and I notice there's a new server to deliver them, just as giggly as the first one. Maybe they're taking turns. She wants a selfie with me, I oblige, and she goes away beaming.

"It's amazing how this place hasn't changed," I muse, looking around. "Same kitsch on the walls, same tables and chairs, same menus."

"Same staff," he points out as a burly man ambles over to us carrying two plates piled high with food. His smile is a mile wide.

"**Y**ou two!" Artie puts our food on the table before throwing his arms around Cole and just about lifting him out of his chair. I can't help but laugh at the surprise and embarrassment practically pouring off my former partner. Artie gives me the same treatment, a little gentler though. "My servers told me you were out here, and there was a cute guy with bedroom eyes sitting with you!"

I laugh at the expression on Cole's face when he hears this. "And you guessed it was him?"

"I didn't dare hope," Artie laughs. "But here you are! It's just like the old days! What are you doing together? Performing again?"

"Oh, no, no, no," I laugh, waving my hands. "Not at all. Just here for something to eat and a little reminiscing. That's it."

He shakes his slightly sweaty head. He's a big guy and sweated so much he had to carry a towel with him in summer. "Come on. You can't tease me like this. You've gotta do just one song. Please?"

I glance at Cole with a *would-you-please-get-us-out-of-this* look.

He clears his throat and opens his palms. "Not this time, Artie. I don't even have a guitar with me, and I can't tell you the last time I played. It's been years. Hell knows if I can still play."

"Nonsense. Music is like riding a bike. You never forget. I have a guitar in back, freshly tuned. You can still pick out a song. Something simple. Please?" He's doing everything but dropping to his knees and wringing his hands.

We look at each other.

Then I shrug and give in gracefully. "Can we eat our food while it's still hot though?" I ask Artie with a wink.

"Yes! Yes, go ahead! Just give me the signal, and I'll tell everybody you're gonna go up there." He practically clicks his heels together as he hurries away.

"Are you serious?" Cole hisses.

"Oh, come on. Who wanted to keep going down Memory Lane?" I tease.

"You were the one who didn't want to draw attention to yourself tonight," he reminds me.

"Yeah, well, I changed my mind."

His eyes crinkle up. "You do know I'm gonna make a complete fool out of myself up there?"

"I'm not expecting you to play a twenty-five-minute guitar solo." I take a big bite out of my burger and pretend I'm not laughing at him. We take our time eating—or, in his case, stalling for time. It's not like we were performing complicated songs back in the day. Finally, Cole wipes his hands and mouth on a napkin.

Artie is standing behind the bar watching us the same as everybody else. I catch his eyes and he makes a beeline for the stage. Oh, jeez. I hope this wasn't a terrible idea. All I need is for somebody to record me looking like an idiot.

"Everybody, everybody!" Artie stands behind the microphone, arms in the air. "I have a surprise for you tonight!"

Just like that, the room explodes. Either they were all hoping I would sing or he's been blabbing to everybody that we agreed to perform. Regardless, the crowd goes wild. I can hardly hear my heart beating in my ears as Cole leads the way to the corner where Artie's waiting with a guitar. I do my little bow and wave to the people crowding the stage.

"Okay, okay. Thank you." I sit on one of the two stools Artie pulled out for us and take a sip of water. Cole, meanwhile, strums a few chords and does a few runs, loosening his fingers. For a man who hasn't played guitar in forever, he sounds pretty good. I wonder if he was telling the truth when he said he hasn't been playing.

When I look over at him, and he smiles at me the way he always used to smile, the years fall away. We might as well be teenagers again. Our whole lives ahead of us. Nothing but hope. And as long as we had each other back then, we had it all.

Then something happens. That old magic. I know he feels it, too.

He strums through the opening chords of Fleetwood Mac's

Landslide and the cheering from the audience tells me it's a good choice. One of our favorites, back in the day. The older folks always loved it, and that was who we normally played for. As an adult, the lyrics have a new meaning for me.

I open my mouth to sing. "Took my love, took it down …"

Cole smiles at me again, and we watch each other as he plays and I sing, and it's just the two of us. Nobody else. The audience blurs, fades. We might as well be the only two people in the world, spinning a web around ourselves. When we reach the chorus, and he takes up the harmony, my heart swells until I'm afraid it might choke me. I keep singing through it all, and by the time the last notes ring out from the guitar, there are tears in my eyes.

"One more. One more," the crowd chants.

"Another?" I mouth, and he nods with a sly grin.

It looks like we're putting on a concert.

TAYLOR

"Thank you! Thank you so much!" We're both breathless, sweaty from the hot lights, and positively glowing with joy.

Cole takes my hand, and we bow together one last time with the sound of riotous, ecstatic cheers almost deafening me. I lost count of the number of songs we did. Fifteen? Twenty, maybe?

It seemed like every time we finished one song, another old favorite came to mind. It flowed naturally. We didn't even have to talk about it. All we had to do was exchange a look, raise an eyebrow.

He'd strike a chord, and I'd smile, and the lyrics would come back even though I haven't sung these kinds of songs for years, ever since we last performed as a duo, as a matter of fact. It's amazing how I don't remember a word of the French I studied for four years, but I have this endless song list in my head.

I'm on Cloud Nine. I can hardly feel the floor under my feet.

I can't stop smiling. I even stop to take selfies with the audience without thinking twice. Normally, I only have so much patience for all the requests for a photo. I guess, I am cynical now. I know most of those photos have a monetary value. They will use them on social media to validate themselves, sell their products, or whatever.

The smile I wear for each photo is more genuine than normal. I made them happy tonight. No, we did. Together. I can't remember the last time I had the chance to connect one-on-one with the fans. When was the last time I was able to speak to a fan, touch them, or know I made their night?

It takes another hour for us to escape the bar, between the photos and hugs and the beers Artie insists on giving us after our impromptu concert.

"It would be rude to say no," Cole reminds me with a boyish grin.

I get the feeling he just wants to savor the moment. His pride won't let him break down and admit what a rush he's feeling, but he doesn't have to explain. I understand too well. I would never rob him of this when he's having such a great time. Still, all good things come to an end, no matter how much fun they are. As my forty-eight hours will eventually end.

I stop in front of Cole's car. "Are you going to drive after drinking?"

"I haven't been *drinking*. I've had three beers all night. Besides this is not LA. The most harm I can do is hit a raccoon."

It's wonderful to slide into the silence and privacy of Cole's glossy dark blue BMW. The entire night has been a happy dream I wish I never had to wake up from.

"You're in a good mood."

"Like you're not! You haven't stopped smiling like a goon since we started performing!"

"I thought Artie was gonna drop dead when we kept going."

"It's a good thing we stopped when we did, or he might have," I say with a laugh. "I'm glad we made him happy." I lean my head against the headrest contentedly.

"You made everybody happy tonight." He smiles that special smile and glances at me in that special way that always used to melt me back in the day. "Including me."

"You? Really? You said you didn't want to perform in the first place."

"Yeah, well, not all of us are used to getting onstage in front of people anymore."

"You must make speeches all the time. Right? I mean, you're a big deal too right. You must have your own business by now. You always wanted to start your own."

His jaw clenches. "I took over my father's business, Taylor."

I stare at him in surprise. "You did? Why? You said you'd never do that."

"Circumstances change. People change." He sighs, tapping his fingers on the steering wheel like he's still picking at guitar strings.

I wonder what circumstances would have made him take over his father's business. He used to despise it. I want to ask him more, but I don't want to pry. It's clear he doesn't want to talk about it.

"Thank you for coming up with me tonight. I know it wasn't easy for you. Getting up there and being vulnerable in front of all those people."

He shrugs. "Yeah, being on stage is not something I am comfortable with, but I wasn't going to let you go up there on your own."

"You were incredible," I say softly.

His right hand stops strumming invisible strings and closes over mine. "Thank you. That was a hell of a lot of fun."

"It was, right? I mean, Jesus, I haven't felt this good after a concert in years. All that good adrenaline is back, you know? That good feeling. I haven't felt that feeling in such a long time. I mean, the adrenaline is always there, but it doesn't make me feel this happy. Keyed-up and happy aren't the same thing." I'm babbling and I know I'm babbling but I can't make sense of, or stop the sensation of feeling so high I'm almost dizzy.

His grip tightens around my fingers. "It doesn't make you happy anymore? Performing?"

"I don't know. Forget it. It's not important. I don't wanna bring down the mood. We just had a great night! What a rush."

"Don't sidestep the question," he murmurs.

I roll my eyes. "Ugh. Do you ever get tired of thinking you know me so well?"

He smiles. "I will as soon as I stop knowing you so well."

I would never admit this if I weren't three beers in, or maybe it's because it's Cole and I trust him with my secrets, but suddenly I'm confessing to stuff that would make my manager's toes curl.

"I guess it's not the way I thought it would be. Being famous, I mean. It's much more complicated. You know, you think you'll make all this money and nobody will ever be able to tell you what to do, ever again. You think it'll give you choices. Really, it seems as if my choices dissolve every time I release an album, every time I've gone on tour. Every dollar I've made for the record company just ties me tighter, and they're the ones holding the rope." I can't meet his eyes. I'm so ashamed. Being famous was what tore us apart, and now I'm telling him it wasn't worth it. I must sound completely insane.

He absorbs this, screwing his mouth up to one side the way he always used to when something was on his mind. "How did you think it would be when you got famous?" His voice soft and tentative as if I am a wild animal that came up to his backyard and he doesn't want to spook me.

I force myself to chuckle like I don't have a care in the world. "How does anybody think it will be? Perfect. Magical. The happy ending, the adoring fans, and buckets of money and tons of freedom. How many people have spent their lives chasing it, right? Seeing my face on TV, hearing my voice on the radio. Appearing at awards shows—getting nominated for a few. Rubbing elbows with other famous people, meeting my childhood crushes. Maybe making one of them fall in love with me."

He laughs, but gently. I didn't fool him for a second. "Sounds like you went from general to pretty specific."

I match his laughter. "Okay, so I had some pretty specific dreams. Sue me."

"It may not have turned out the way you thought it would, but it looks great on the surface, though."

"Yeah. On the surface. That's the thing. As long as everybody thinks it's great, things are perfect, and the whole fame myth gets perpetuated all over again. That's how it rolls."

"You sound much more cynical than you used to."

"I'm not a kid anymore. I had to grow up. Fast."

His eyes narrow to dangerous slits. "You didn't have to do anything you didn't want to, did you?"

"No, no, nothing like that. I guess I'm maybe a little burned out? Maybe it's all too much? Tonight, I remembered how simple it can be. How much fun singing actually is. I miss when it was fun. And the connection. And Artie's burgers."

"They still make a good burger there, don't they?" he murmurs.

"Oh, God, yes. Just what I needed. The whole night's been just what I needed." I look at him again. "Thank you for that."

He lifts my hand to his lips and places a soft, tender kiss on my knuckles. The chill that runs down my spine is something I've missed, too. I've missed it a lot. It wasn't until I felt his touch and his kiss again that I figured out how much I've been missing that special feeling. He's the only man I've ever felt anything real for. My pulse picks up speed when the car turns down my street. *My street*. Wow, what a strange thought. It's not my street. Or, it won't be once I sell the house. I'm selling the house.

Am I selling the house?

Of course, I am.

I frown. Until today I was so sure I was selling it. It could be because I haven't been this happy in such a long time. Now I'm thinking: what if I didn't? If I just kept it, just in case I want to return one day.

I'm so mixed up between the giggly giddiness still coursing through me that I miss the figure sitting on the porch when we pull up in front of the garage. It doesn't help that the light above the door isn't on. Cole helps me out of the car, and we are both a little buzzed, a little high on joy, as he bends down to kiss me. I return the kiss enthusiastically. Maybe a little too enthusiastically.

"Taylor?"

We both jump at the sound of a male voice, and I spin around to find the dark figure sitting in the rocking chair. He stands and takes a step forward, letting the light from the street lamp fall on his face. I put a hand on my chest and let out a shaky breath. He should be careful. For a second there I was ready to pull out my Mace and blind the sucker.

"Simon? What are you doing here?"

Cole looks down at me. "You know this guy?"

"Who the hell is this?" Simon shouts, jabbing a finger in Cole's direction. Cole's jaw tightens just the way his hand tightens around mine.

We were having such a good night, too.

"Guess what? Brian asked me out," I say.

Cole whips his head around. "What?"

"Brian Stopps from my class. You know, he plays football."

"I know who he is. He's a jock," he says tightly.

"He's not a jock. He's actually a pretty cool guy."

"What did you say to him?" His voice is quiet and his face expressionless.

I stare at him curiously. "I said yes."

His body is suddenly very still. "Why?"

"What do you mean why?" I ask, a frown on my face.

"Why did you say yes? Do you like him?"

I shrug. "I don't know. I guess so."

A strange expression crosses his face, as if he is in pain.

I take a step closer towards him. "What's the matter with you? Are you all right?"

He turns away from me. "I'm fine."

I walk up to him and put my hand on his tense shoulder. He whirls around, his eyes blazing, a white band around his mouth. "I don't want you going out with snot-nosed, fancy pants Brian."

I shake my head, astonished. Brian hasn't been snot-nosed since we were in first grade. "Why ever not?"

His hands clench hard. "Because you should be going out with me."

My jaw drops. "You mean … like boyfriend and girlfriend?"

He scowls. "Yes. Would that be so bad?"

I look at him. Really look at him. At the liquid gold and green eyes, the thick eyelashes, the dark shock of hair falling over his forehead, and the full lips. So red it is almost as if he is wearing lipstick. My gaze travels down the strong column of his throat and his broad shoulders. He is easily the best-looking kid in town and most of my friends are crazy about him. My gaze travels up to his eyes. They are molten with some strange emotion.

For a second we stare at each other, then he grabs me by the shoulders and presses his mouth to mine. I'm too shocked to respond at first. I just about manage to breathe. His Abercrombie Fierce cologne fills my nostrils and a funny thing happens. Butterflies start fluttering madly in my stomach and my heart races. A strange excitement zips around my body making me feel almost dizzy with it.

His mouth softens on mine.

His hands come up to brush my throat, my face, then they are in my hair. I forget everything, the world stops spinning. I melt into him. When he raises his head, I stare at him with my mouth open.

"Be my girl?" he asks, his voice as smooth as dark chocolate.

It is impossible for me to speak so I just nod. That was the beginning of us.

COLE

PRESENT DAY

I t's like a switch flips in my head.

One minute, I was happier and more excited than I could remember being in a long time. Eight years, maybe? I was holding Taylor's hand and planning on taking her inside and screwing her brains out again. Now, I'm ready to kill the bastard standing in front of me. All she needs to do is ask me and I will pulverize him with a song in my heart.

"Simon," Taylor says, a hint of irritation creeping into her voice. "I asked you a question. What are you doing here? I didn't ask you to come." Her eyes sweep the street, back and forth, like she's looking out for paparazzi, or the random passerby with a cell. I wonder vaguely, in the background of my rage, what it must be like to always have to think about that.

"I had to see you."

She shakes her head, half in disbelief. "Why? Wait ... how did you find me?"

"Nick told me."

She scowls. "Looks like I need a new manager because he shouldn't have. I made it very clear that I wanted to have some time away from the rat race."

"I'm not the rat race. I care about you."

"You don't care about me, Simon. We're a PR stunt."

He looks sheepish. "Yeah. Well, it doesn't have to be." He leans on the porch rail with the closest thing to an expression of caring he can probably muster. He looks like the most insincere piece of shit I've ever seen and I would love nothing more than to cave his face in.

"Do you want me to get him out of here?" I murmur. Her hand is still in mine.

His eyes flick back to me. "Who's this asshole?"

"I hope you didn't just call me an asshole." My voice is a low, deadly growl. I hope for his sake that he doesn't think about underestimating me. All the years I've spent in kickboxing and cross training aren't for nothing. Meanwhile, he looks like he's strung-out on designer drugs. Skinny, pale, sunken eyes.

"Why? What you gonna do about it?" he challenges from behind the wooden rail.

"Okay, okay. Let's go inside before this gets even more stupid." Taylor shakes her head in disgust and leads me into the house. I wait just next to her, at her elbow, as she unlocks the door. I won't let her out of my sight around an ass like this guy. Besides, he needs to know she's mine.

"Sit." She points to the couch, then folds her arms and leans against the wall. He's like a puppy dog. He goes right over there and sinks into the cushions, looking up at her with those dead eyes of his.

"So who's the hick?" he asks sulkily. "I don't recognize him from anywhere."

I cringe inwardly for him. The shallow world she lives in sickens me. A world where you are nothing unless you are a celebrity. He pushes limp blond hair out of his eyes. The whole floppy hair trend needs to go away. How can women even think that's hot?

Taylor sighs. "Cole, this is Simon. He's the lead singer of The Screamers."

I cough to cover up my laugh. The Screamers? Doesn't say much for his voice. "Never heard of them," I say with a shrug. It's the truth, too. My musical taste doesn't lean toward hard rock, which he's obviously deep into. He looks appalled.

"Simon, this is my best friend, Cole. I've known him for a long time. He was my partner for years, back when I first started out." She glances at me, a warning glance. *Don't tell him anything else about us*, that glance says. Is she afraid of him? My blood starts to boil. She called their relationship a PR stunt.

He barely looks my way before pleading with her again. "Baby, I couldn't believe it when you ran out on me like that."

She rolls her eyes. "First of all, don't call me that. I'm not your baby. I've never been your baby. That's what you've wanted, but not me."

He throws a sly look in my direction. "Oh, come on. We had fun together."

She holds up one finger. "Are you trying to suggest there is something between us for Cole's benefit, because you and I both know there is nothing going on between us. Why you made this mad trip in the middle of the night is completely beyond me."

"Why can't you just give us a chance? We'd be good together."

"It would never work between us, and I've told you that a million times. If you want to be friends, I'm fine with that. You can't follow me around like this. I wanted some time on my own."

"But you're not alone, are you?" he asks with a smirk.

I can see her start to fume. I'm fuming, too. What a loser this douchebag is. Can't get over a woman, so he follows her around with a broken heart. Granted, Taylor isn't just any woman. She's one of a kind, extraordinary. And the best lay I've ever had, hands down. But stalking her? That's taking it too far. I hate the thought of her even letting him near her.

"She doesn't want you here." I take a step forward, sliding my arms out of my jacket. "I think it's time for you to go."

"What are you gonna do?" he asks, still smirking. "You gonna throw me out, tough guy?"

As I get closer I can see that his pupils are huge. He's obviously high on something. "If I have to. Yeah. I will pull you physically from that couch, open the door and throw your ass out onto the sidewalk. Please, give me the chance to do that."

"Cole," Taylor warns from behind me, but my blood is roiling. It's obvious that being nice isn't working on this guy. I'm going to do things my way.

"Come on. What'll it be? You get out of here on your own two feet, or you force me to throw you out?" I start rolling up my sleeves.

"Go on and touch me," the prick sneers. "You have no idea what I could do to you. My lawyer would be on your ass in a minute."

A laugh rumbles out of my throat. To my surprise, it's genuine. "That's great. My legal team would love to meet your lawyer. It would be a nice break from the international negotiations they're working on right now. Like a vacation, almost." I go to him and clamp a hand around his way-too-scrawny bicep, hauling him to his feet. "Let's go."

He's obviously a lover and not a fighter, because he calls out to Taylor over his shoulder, "Taylor, I love you. Don't you get that?"

COLE

I swear I want to laugh. It's like one of those crazy romantic comedies. She doesn't answer, and I open the door and toss Simon outside, just like I promised. I dust my hands. "If I ever hear about you bothering her again or if you even look her way when she doesn't want you to, we'll be seeing each other. And next time, that legal team I told you about will be with me. It'll be a blast." I slam the door in his face, then flip the lock.

It doesn't hit me until just then that she might not have wanted me to be so forceful with him. She said she wanted to be friends, right? Women are different about that kind of thing. Me? I'd tell him to fuck off and never speak to him again.

She's still standing where I left her, against the wall, arms crossed. I can't read her expression.

"Sorry, but that guy's bad news," I say with a shrug. "You can't expect me to meet somebody like him and not want to kill him just for touching you. I took it easy on him. I could probably snap him like a dry twig."

She opens her mouth like she wants to speak, but no words come out. Shit. Just when things were going well. It looks like she's spoiling for a fight, which come to think of it is just fine. I like her kicking and clawing anyway and we'll just end it the way the way I like to end all my fights with her.

Maybe I don't know her as well as I used to anymore because she throws herself into my arms, and wraps her hands around my neck in a death grip. "Thank you!"

This is unexpected. "You're happy about this?"

"Are you kidding? I've wanted to do that for years! I just don't have the upper body strength."

I laugh. "I thought you were about to bitch me out for being an overprotective, jealous meathead."

Her eyes go wide, then narrow as she practically purrs. "What if I like overprotective, jealous meatheads?"

"Oh, yeah? Why didn't you say so?" In a flash, I bend down and throw her over my shoulder. She squeals and giggles, half-heartedly fighting me off as I carry her up the stairs. By the time I drop her onto the bed, she's not laughing anymore. Instead, she takes me by the arms and pulls me down until I'm on top of her and we're kissing and touching, and it's even better than before because I'm hyped up after our performance together and I know she is too.

My veins are full of fire.

I slide one hand under her sweater, and I know I'll never get enough of touching her soft, smooth skin. Once I asked her how she gets it that smooth and she laughed and joked that she bathed in asses milk. She was always like a fantasy come true. From the first day I found her in the treehouse.

She writhes and sighs, arching her back, asking for more without saying a word. My hand closes over her breast and I squeeze gently, hardening when she moans into my mouth. I feel her nipple hardening against my palm. My fingertips dance over the lace trimming the cup of her bra and she strains upward until I pull the cup down to trace slow circles around that tight nipple with my thumb.

I break our kiss to run my mouth over her jaw and down her neck. Her pulse races under my tongue as I taste her. She's so sweet. Her fingers run through my hair and she holds my head close. I take the hint and kiss her harder, letting her scent and taste and the sound of her sighs pull me under until I don't know anymore where I end and she begins. She's always been part of me. I know that now.

I take my time undressing her, exploring every inch of her body. I want to give her every bit of pleasure she can handle and more. I want her to scream my name and beg me to stop because she doesn't think her body can take it, then push her farther than she's ever gone. I want her to need me the way I need her.

"Cole … yes …" Her eyes are closed, her head rolling from side to side as I peel off her panties and settle between her thighs. Her heat calls to me, drawing me in, promising bliss. She runs her hands under the back of my shirt, pulling it up over my head, kissing my shoulders and chest and arms. I close my eyes and let the pressure from her lips erase the past, the empty years spent without her. It's like half my heart was missing all this time.

Her legs tighten around my waist, and I'm just about ready to break the zipper on my jeans, I'm so hard and aching to be inside her again. She claws at my shoulders and back, breathing heavy, moaning and whispering and begging for more. "Please … take me …" she whispers, staring up into my eyes. "I need you inside me, Cole … please …"

I strip off my pants, my hands shaking with urgency. I can't breathe, I can't even think about anything but sinking deep into her. Her eyes practically glow in the dark, staring into my soul, mouth open as she gasps when I slide home and bury my length in her tight sheath.

This is what I need. This is all I've ever needed. The two of us, together as one, moving in sync as we push each other higher. Her legs wrap around my hips and pull me deeper, her hands moving up and down my back, gripping my ass, clawing my neck and shoulders the first time she comes. "So good …" she whispers in my ear between gasps for breath.

It *is* so good. She's right about that.

I push up on my hands and look down at her moving under me, undulating like a wave in time with my thrusts. She stretches up to brush her lips against mine, whimpering, and I return her kiss. We move slowly, grinding against each other, working together the way we did onstage. We don't have to talk things through.

We just know each other.

I want to savor this. I want it to go on forever, the perfection of our bodies wrapped up together, the sound of her moans and the way she cries out my name as she comes, pulsing around my length, begging me to follow her.

I can't. Not yet.

I clench my jaw and close my eyes and hold on until she calms down, then start again.

"Oh, God!" she gasps, trembling, "Yes! Please, Cole ... please ...!" She jerks her hips in time with my thrusts and picks up speed. I follow her now, letting her drive me as crazy as I've been driving her. I slide my arms under her shoulders and roll onto my back, still inside her.

She rocks her hips back and forth, faster and faster. I can't hold back anymore. I'm past the point of no return now. I take her by the waist and hold her still, as I slam into her with deep, hard thrusts. She throws her head back, her cries become louder and louder the closer she gets. I watch her breasts bouncing, her hair trailing over my fingers. Everything is her, all around me. I'm lost. She's all that exists.

I feel her tightening around me again and I know she's as close as I am. We move in a blur, faster and faster until we explode in each other's arms and she collapses on top of me, shaking.

"Oh ... oh, God ... Cole ..." Her voice shakes as hard as her body. A fierce joy fills my body to know I'm the reason she's a wreck now. I did that.

Her hair is damp with sweat. I smooth it back from her forehead and press my lips against her overheated skin. "You okay?" I ask.

"I feel like my heart's about to pound out of my chest, but otherwise? Yeah. I'm fine." She smiles before kissing me. We stay in each other's arms, the air heavy with the smell of sex.

If only I could stop this moment from ending, then we would never end.

I touch the moisture on her cheek. She tells me it is sweat, though it looks a lot like tears. She turns her face away before I can ask again if she's all right.

TAYLOR

17 YEARS OLD

I don't dress fancy for most occasions, but today is different. I sit in front of my mirror and carefully apply a thin coat of mascara to my eyelashes. My stepmother appears in the doorway of my bedroom.

"Do you need any help?" she asks.

I turn to look at her with surprise. She has had no interest in my life, or development until now. I walk to the door. Even at this moment I can feel the hate radiating out of her. "No, thanks. I need to get dressed," I tell her before shutting the door gently. She can't wait to see me gone. Well, I won't let her drain my excitement. I will be gone. She is welcome to this house.

Calmly I walk over to my closet and pull a long, sleek black plastic protector from the hanging rod. Holding it above my head I go over to the bed and lay it flat. I unzip the case, revealing the most beautiful cold-shoulder, red dress I have ever purchased. I am obsessed with the single shoulder style and I couldn't believe how perfect it was when I saw it in the shop window. I used the money I saved from all the gigs I've worked in the past year. Even so I didn't have enough to afford it, but Cole insisted on helping pay for half, so I managed to buy it two months ago.

I look at the dress before me and my smile widens tenfold. I've dreamed about this moment my entire life and it's finally happening. At one of our wdeekly performances at Artie's, a local bar/restaurant, a recording company representative who was passing through heard us. He asked if Cole and I would audition for a record deal. A bigwig would be travelling down specially to see us. And now, we must nail the audition to have a chance.

I slip into the dress, which reaches a little above my knees. It hugs the curves of my body in all the right places and makes me look like I'm all grown-up. Suddenly, I feel nervous and light-headed. This is my big moment. The opportunity I have been waiting for all my life. What if I don't make it? All my dreams will be shattered.

I grab my phone, hit Cole's number, and put it on speaker while I slip into my high-heeled shoes. We're supposed to meet in the choir hall at the school, but I need to hear his voice. Cole has always been an expert at keeping me calm.

It rings multiple times before going to voicemail, and my heart pounds a little louder in my ears. I am teeming with nervousness, excitement, and fear. I go and stand in front of the mirror.

My eyes are bright and my face looks pale. I quickly rub a little blusher into the apple of my cheeks. Then I straighten my shoulders. Why should I be nervous? Singing is what I do best. Even if I mess up, I will never give up. As soon as I turn eighteen I will leave this house and find my fortune. No matter what I will become famous.

I try calling Cole once more to no avail. I hear Rebecca, my friend's car honk outside. Shaking my head and staring at my illuminated phone screen, I open my bedroom door and make my way to the front door.

"Good luck. It's your great dream so I hope they give you a contract," I hear from behind me.

I turn toward my stepmother. In that moment, I realize I don't hate her. I don't even blame her for hating me. My dad shouldn't have forced her to take custody of me. It was not fair.

"Thank you," I respond and walk out the door.

On the way to the school, I am too hyped to even make conversation with Rebecca. My heart races and my hands shake. Rebecca pulls into the school and I take a deep breath. Seeing Cole's car in the car park calms me slightly, but I need him. He's my anchor.

Rebecca asks if I need a lift back, but I tell her Cole will take me home. Then I open the car door and make my way to the front door of the school. There I stop dead in my tracks, my hand on the cool metal handle.

"There's something I think I should tell you," Cole says.

My head pops up from where I was resting it on his chest. "Oh, no. You're pregnant."

His laughter rings through the bedroom. "You got me. I was gonna pretend the baby was yours and use you for child support for the next eighteen years."

"I'm too smart for you." I grin.

His smile fades a little, but not entirely. "Seriously. There's something I want to talk about."

Hmm. Seriously, huh? I don't know if I like the sound of this. Conversations that start like this don't go well for me, historically. I sit up, pulling myself from the delicious warmth of his embrace, gathering the blankets around me. "What is it?" I ask in a tight whisper.

"Hey, it's nothing bad—at least, I don't think it's bad. I may be jumping the gun a bit, but I can't pretend it's not there."

Relief makes me laugh. "What's not there?"

He reaches for me, sliding a gentle hand down the side of my face, over my shoulder, down my arm. "The complete certainty that I can't let you go. Not again."

I gasp. No, that's not what I expected at all. "Oh, Cole."

"I don't want to scare you off, but—"

I take his hand in both of mine. "A part of me is wildly happy, but another part of me is terrified. After what happened the last time."

He snatches his hand out of my grip and lays two fingers against my lips to silence me, shaking his head, his eyes full of sadness and remorse. "Can we not talk about the past for once. I was just a kid, Taylor. I made the wrong choice. Everyone deserves a second chance. Even me." He pauses and takes a deep breath. "I'm a man now. I know exactly what I want. And that is you."

"But how? My life is in LA and yours is here."

"I don't know yet how we will sort this, but if it's what you want too, I'll make it happen. I promise you that."

I pull away from him. My heart is so heavy. I should be exploding with joy. He wants me. He doesn't want to let me go. He just said so himself, but I can't forget how easily he let me go the last time. How little his promises meant. He was my whole world and I truly thought nothing could break us up. But he shattered that trust and I don't know how to repair it. It is like a broken antique vase that you stick back together because you can't bear to throw something so rare and valuable away, but all the crack lines are still there to remind you of the time it smashed on the ground. To tell you that it has lost all its value.

"What is it?" he asks huskily.

I cover my face with one hand. I can't show him my vulnerability or my pain and hurt that in the end, everyone I ever loved abandoned me. I just can't trust anyone. Especially, him.

"Taylor?" he prompts.

"Nothing. I'm just not good at relationships. I've been a mess for such a long time."

"A mess?" He sits up and his tone of voice changes to one of raw concern. "What do you mean? You're the least messy person I know."

I stare at him from between my fingers. He looks so sincere, so worried about me. I let my hand fall from my face and my voice is flat. "You've only been with me for a day, Cole. There's a lot you don't know."

"Is there something I don't know about? Something unhealthy, maybe?" He's trying to be subtle, but I know what he means. It's the business I am in. Simon is a good representative of the kind of people who populate show business.

"No, it's not that. I'm not, like, blowing thousands a week, and shooting it in my arm or anything. I don't even drink very much. I'm probably the only person I know who doesn't. Sometimes they act like I'm from another planet, or like I think I'm better than them. I'm sure there are some who assume I'm in recovery. I don't care if that's what they think, as long as they leave me alone about it."

"So what's the problem, then? You live a good life, you're responsible, you have the world at your fingertips. Why are you in a mess?"

I sit there, blinking, mute with disbelief. Can he be this naïve? He's such a savvy person otherwise, Mr. CEO, Mr. Confident. Mr. I Walk Into A Room And Panties Melt. He just doesn't understand because it didn't happen to him. He was not the person with the broken heart. Oh, what will my therapist think when she hears about me diving headfirst into old patterns?

"Come on, babe. What's really on your mind? You know you can tell me. You can tell me anything."

I know he means it, too, which somehow makes it worse. He wants me to feel comfortable opening up to him, even when there's no way to put my feelings into words.

He frowns and falls silent for a while. Then, he asks, "Are you disappointed? Is it too much pressure?"

There is so much I want to say: I want to say, *No, until I was with you tonight, up there onstage, even I didn't' know what it was. You're the piece I've been missing all along. Ever since that day at the audition, when I lost you, I lost the real reason I loved perform-ing. Nothing is as fun as it used to be.*

In the beginning when everything was still so new and there was so much to see and learn, I could fool myself into thinking all my dreams were coming true. When that got old, and it did very quickly, I realized I didn't feel fulfilled. Something was missing. I told myself I was being immature and ungrateful, that I was one of the luckiest girl's alive. I was living my dream and there were millions of girls out there who would give their right arm to be in my situation.

So I should just damn well get over myself.

Well, you proved tonight that there is nothing to get over. I'm not immature or ungrateful. I was the little goat who was starving to death while everyone around me was filling my plate with fillet mignon. You were what I needed. When you turned your back on me and left me alone, you took away everything that ever really mattered.

But I don't say any of these things.

"Pretty much," I whisper over the sound of my aching heart. I can't tell him what I'm really feeling. He would never understand.

When he reaches for me, I let myself rest in his arms. It's been so long since I've had the chance to rest, to really rest. No pretense, no façade. I can be myself. I can relax and let it all go.

"You know," he whispers as his hand gently strokes my hair. So soothing. "You don't have to do this if you don't want to. You're a grown woman, and you probably have plenty of money by now. I hope you've been smart with it."

"Of course. Super smart. I'm doing well."

"That's great. See? You don't have to keep recording and touring. You can retire. Pursue something else. You're young, you have the rest of your life to do what you really want to do. And if you feel like playing housewife I'm in the market for one of those too," he says with a wry smile.

I love performing with you, but you already told me years ago that you don't need it. You're already rich, right? I will myself not to go stiff in his arms and give myself away. "I love performing though," I say softly.

"So, perform on your terms. You're the boss. Do what you want, sing what you want, where and when you want. You're famous. Anybody would be happy to book you. You'll pull in huge crowds."

"I have contracts. I can't walk out on them. Trust me, I won't be nearly as comfortable anymore if I do that. If I had balls, they'd have me by them."

He looks deep into my eyes. "Taylor, do you need money, because what's mine is yours. Just say the word and—"

"No," I say quickly. "I don't need your money. I enjoy earning my own money."

"Okay. Step back when you can. As soon as possible. I believe in you. You can do this." When he says it like that, with his mouth against the top of my head and his strong arms holding me close, I can almost believe him. I can just step off the Fame Machine and be with him. I can imagine a life with him, away from the public eye. Maybe a house somewhere pretty, with a garden I can tend to and a room I can use as a library. We can curl up with a blanket and a cup of tea in that room on rainy days. I can enjoy my life. I can just about see it if I squeeze my eyes closed tight enough.

I can't walk around with my eyes closed all the time, now, can I?

"Thank you for believing in me the way you do," I whisper. It's all I can say. It sounds lame, trite, but I feel like I have to say something. I wish I could tell him the truth. Things are going so well, the threat of pushing him away and losing the beautiful moment we're in is enough to shut my mouth.

We stay that way for a long time until our breathing falls in sync and the only thing I can hear is his heart beating under my ear. His strong, steady heartbeat. It lulls me into a deep, soft sleep full of dreams. For once, they're beautiful dreams. Dreams of love and fulfillment, connection to somebody other than another lost soul like me. Somebody real, somebody substantial, somebody I can lean on when I need a little extra strength. Somebody like Cole. I dream about loving Cole, and him loving me.

COLE

I wake up to the sensation of something delicate trailing on my shoulder. I open my eyes and look into Taylor's face. I look around me in confusion. The whole place is lit with candles and Taylor is wearing a white babydoll nightie. For a few seconds, I think I'm still asleep and dreaming.

Then she smiles, a slow sexy smile. I touch her hair. It is gleaming in the flickering candlelight. "One day, do you think you can grow your hair back to how it was?"

She smiles. "Like Rapunzel?"

"The way it was before. Sometimes I dream that we are teenagers again and we're in your treehouse, your gold hair is spread out under your body. It was so beautiful, Taylor. You were like a living angel on that dark wood."

"Yeah?"

"Yeah."

"Maybe, I'll grow it back."

"Did you wake up because you were horny?"

She nods slowly.

"You wanted something in particular, didn't you?"

She nods again, her cheeks flushing.

"Give me a show, Taylor. You know I can never ever get enough of looking at your body."

I watch hungrily as she gets off the bed and goes to stand in front of me. Slowly and sensuously, she begins to gyrate while lifting the edges of her babydoll gear. I catch a glimpse of white cotton panties. They are tight and show the shape of her pussy. Suddenly, I am rock hard. She slips her fingers into the waistband of her panties and drags them down her thighs. Now she is bare under the transparent nightie. She turns around and bends from the waist. With all the stage work she is very limber. It's the first time in eight years since I've seen Taylor's pussy from this angle.

I nearly lose it.

Her pussy pouts beneath her lush bottom. Fuck, she's so turned on, her slit is practically steaming with her juices. She turns her head, looks at me. Her eyes are ablaze with sexual lust, with a power-lust as well. She knows, right now, she has me wrapped up around her little finger, exactly where she wants me.

She wriggles her butt suggestively, and I swear, I've never wanted to run face first into anything so much in my life. The urge to grab that nubile body and ram my cock into her is almost more than I can bear, but I asked for a show, so I force myself to lie there and just drool at my proud beauty while she does her thing … and drives me insane.

Utterly naked, she crawls towards me on her hands and knees. I grab her by her waist, haul her up, and sit her on my chest. Slowly, she rubs her wet pussy on my body. The sweet smell of her intoxicates me. She swings herself around, deliberately raising one leg over my head in a graceful, dancer's arc, giving me a completely unobstructed and very, very close view of her glistening pussy. She lets me ogle it for a few seconds before ending her maneuver.

A soft hand reaches for my cock and strokes it with maddening slowness, tracing each vein, her fingers whispering over the stretched skin. She bends forward and wraps her warm mouth over my cockhead. My balls clench with anticipation. Her soft fingers cup and squeeze my sack. Devilishly she drags her fingernails with torturous slowness along the tender skin. Delicately, her mouth moves down my shaft and I groan as I feel the silk of her mouth bathing every inch of me.

All the way down.

I feel my cockhead slip into the heat of her throat. Until her nose is buried in the nest of my pubic hair. She sucks me until it is clear to her that anymore of that and I will shoot my load. She lets my cock slide out of her mouth and turns back to look at me. Her expression is intense. "I want your cock in my ass, Cole. I kept it for you all these years. I want you to stretch me again. Stretch me to my limit."

Then she leans forward and picks up a bottle of oil that she has left by the bedside and hands it to me. Then she gets back on her hands and knees and waits for me. I move forward, my cock aching, and she squirms. Her pussy is dripping and her thighs are slick, but it is not her pussy she wants me to service. My hand trembles as I reach out to caress the soft

86

skin of her ass. It's been so long. So long. Goose bumps rise on her skin and run down her thighs. Slowly, I open her cheeks and expose her tiny rose. I love looking at her puckered little hole. It is so pretty.

As she feels the heat of my gaze she moans with impatience. I can feel her trembling as she pushes her ass backward. I lift the bottle and pour a steady stream of oil over the crack. She freezes. I smear the oil over my finger. Very gently I push the finger into her.

She screams and her body begins to shake. As my finger slips into her body, her hole begins to pulse. I know what it wants. It wants to be stretched. She stays very still as I pull out of her. My finger comes out with a popping sound. Her ass closes in on itself.

"Hurry," she whispers fiercely, mad with desire. She has to have it inside her.

She stays very still while I separate her cheeks and center the tip of my throbbing cock at her entrance. My cock looks way too big to enter her. Her hole looks impossibly small and defenseless to take me in.

"Cole, please, get inside me," she begs.

She makes a strange animal sound of pain as the bulbous head of my cock tries to penetrate her. The muscles of her sphincter resist and I become still. The head is always the most difficult. I see her take a deep breath and relax her body, before pushing back against the head of my cock. The crown slips in, her breath comes out in a great rush, and her muscles grip my cock in a warm hug.

Slowly, her anal canal opens to welcome me deeper into her

body as I slide in succulent inch by succulent inch. When my balls become wet from contact with her wet pussy, I stop moving and allow her to get used to the intrusion.

My whole cock is inside her, and the only sound in the room is the sound of her harsh breathing. Slowly, I begin to move inside her hot canal.

"I'm ready," she groans.

She has adjusted and I no longer have to go slow or be gentle. I pull out almost to the tip and ram all the way back in. She screams not in pain, but pure pleasure. The nerve endings inside her are being stimulated. Sweat streams down my temples as I begin to thrust faster and faster until I'm pounding into her tight ass without any reservations. I'm so horny taking her sweet ass that I can't hold back. Reaching forward I start playing with her soaking clit.

"Cum in my ass," she grunts as I feel her going over the edge.

Just at that my cock swells up and pumps thick sperm deep inside her as she screams out her own climax. Every intense convulsion milks my cock. She shudders as my hot cum pours into her. When the last of my seed has been squeezed out into her overflowing canal I lean forward and kiss her neck gently.

I love you, I want to say, but I don't. There is no rush. I have always loved her and always will.

The right time will come.

Until it does I'll take it slow and easy.

TAYLOR

17 YEARS OLD

"Cole?" I ask, immediately recognizing the shape of the person lurking in the shadows. "What are you doing out here? It's cold."

His back faces me and he sways from side to side. "Do you actually think we can do this?" he asks. I notice a slur in his voice and my jaw drops.

"Are you … drunk?" I gasp, charging in his direction. I grab his arm and spin him around to face me. Jesus Christ, he is so drunk he can barely stand. His breath reeks of alcohol. I've never seen him like this before. "What the hell, Cole?"

"This is a big recording studio. We don't have a chance," he slurs, losing his balance and using the wall to keep himself upright. I grab him around the waist and attempt to hold him up. My mind is spinning with shock.

"Why do you think that?" I ask, staring at him with astonishment. This is not him. No way. He is always the one who thinks we can reach for the sky.

Cole shakes his head and grabbing me pushes me into the wall he was using to keep himself upright. I stand between his unsteady figure and the concrete wall, my lovely dress getting crushed. "Why don't we just leave and try again another time. It's not like it matters."

"It's not like it matters?" I echo in disbelief. "We've practiced every day for years and have never taken a day off. Even when I lost my voice, we worked on writing a new song. We can do this. Where's your guitar? If we don't go in now, we're going to be late," I say, trying to push him backward. This is unlike him. He has always been so supportive, but something has changed.

He pushes me back into the wall when I try to escape and I notice his eyes for the first time since seeing him. They don't even look like his eyes. They are bloodshot and dead. The only distinguishable emotion within them is lust. "I left it at home. I'm not doing this, Taylor," he says.

I gawk at him, then push him away harder this time, not caring if I knock him off balance. He deserves it for chickening out on me. "What the hell is the matter with you? Why are you doing this now?" I shout.

"I saw the light, Taylor."

I shake my head. "Light? What light?"

"I don't want to do this."

"But this is our big dream. Our big chance."

"This isn't *our* big dream. It's yours. I'm already rich and I don't give a shit about being famous," he says, not meeting my eyes. "If you want it that badly you can do it alone."

My mind spins. I have never felt so betrayed. I shake my head and take a step away from him. "If that's how you really feel why did you pretend all this while and lead me on?" I begin.

Something flashes in his eyes. "I didn't pretend. I just changed my mind."

"Well, I won't make you do anything you don't want to do." I am hardly able to keep my tears at bay as I push past my best friend, or rather my ex-best friend. Even then, I can't leave, I turn around one last time. "Are you sure, Cole? Because you can't change your mind."

"I won't change my mind," he says, his voice hard.

Then something occurs to me. I lift my hand towards him. "Look, if you're nervous, we'll sing something simple. We don't have to do the new song."

He laughs harshly. "Don't you get it, Taylor? I'm not nervous. I just don't want to be your sidekick anymore."

"What about all your promises to take care of me and love me forever?" I whisper.

He can't meet my eyes. "I was kid. What the hell did I know?" he mutters, turning his face away from me.

His words are like a knife in my chest. I turn away from him then. I walk to the hall, my heart bleeding. For a second I stand outside the choir hall doors, brushing my hands down my dress.

If he isn't here for me, I'll be here for myself. I'm not canceling my once in a lifetime opportunity because of him. I stand outside the audition room doors and take a deep breath. Even without Cole in my life, I plan on making something of myself. I'm not giving up on my dream. I'm leaving this god forsaken town and reaching for the stars.

I don't need him. I don't need anybody. Fuck him. I'll make it on my own. One day I'll become a big star. He'll be sorry then. He'll want me back, but I'll spit in his face. Taking a deep breath, I grasp the handle of the door and walk inside. A big fake smile on my face.

COLE

I have appointments this morning. At the very least I should call and ask my secretary to cancel. Isn't that what people do? They meet up with their long-lost loves, reconnect and hell, they might even perform in front of a hundred people or so. Then get back to real life because real life doesn't end just because they like the way a woman's hair smells. The way she smiles. The way she laughs. The way she exists.

I lie there in Taylor's bed and stare at the ceiling. She's in my arms, still asleep, drooling a little on my chest. I don't even care. I'm the guy who normally kicks a woman out of bed roughly forty-five seconds after I'm finished. I'd let her drown me in her drool if it meant spending more time with her.

I watch as dappled light filters into the bedroom through the leaves on the trees outside the window. I can see the shadows dancing above us. If I lie here long enough, holding her the way I am, it's possible that the rest of my life will fall away and go on without me. I'll be able to be with her, just this way, as long as we both live.

It's incredible. I had money, power, respect, social standing, but life was boring and meaningless. I told myself I had it all under control, the way I always do. Everything scheduled, contained, categorized. To be honest, I was almost content with that control. I convinced myself I didn't need anything else. Then she came back to town and here I am, willing to walk away from it all for her.

I won't let her go again. Never. It was hard enough the first time. I'm grabbing this second chance with both hands.

She stirs and rubs her eyes. While she's doing that, I wipe the drool off my bare chest with the corner of the sheet before she sees it. Yet another thing I wouldn't do for anybody else.

"Good morning," she whispers in a sweet, sleepy voice. "God, I must look a mess. I didn't even take off my makeup."

She looks beautiful. Perfect. Even with the smudged mascara and messy hair. "Don't worry about it. You look great."

Her cheeks turn pink like magic. "It's cramped on this bed, isn't it? How did you sleep?"

Like hell, because I couldn't stop thinking about you long enough to fall asleep for more than a few minutes at a time. "Great. You?"

"Fantastic. Best night's sleep I've had in years."

She's not lying the way I am, either. God, everything's so perfect. Why can't things be like this all the time? Why did we have to miss all the years together? I remember why, and bitterness swells up in my chest. It's better not to think about that.

Instead, I smile. "What do you wanna do today?"

Her mouth falls open a little as she blinks in surprise. "Uh, I don't know. I hadn't really thought about it." She pushes her hair around with her hands. An old nervous gesture. "I don't want you to feel like you have to spend time with me if you have other things to do."

"I don't feel like I have to do anything. I want to do this. I want to be with you today—that is, if you want to." What's this cautious dance we're doing? Moving around each other, being careful, taking our time to make sure we don't step on each other's toes. Eight years will do that, I guess. We have to relearn the steps.

Her eyes light up. "Sure, I would love to hang out again. What do you wanna do?"

Good question. I didn't think things through that far. "I don't know. It looks like a beautiful day outside."

She looks out at the blue, cloudless sky. "It does. We should get out and do something."

"I thought you wanted to avoid the public."

"I didn't say we have to go to the mall or anything."

"Damn. I really wanted to go shopping today, too. There's a great shoe sale going on."

"As much as I hate to make you miss a really good bargain ..." The next thing I know, I'm ducking the small pillow she swings at me and I'm picking up a pillow and hitting her with it. Before long, we're both on the floor rolling around, wrestling and laughing just like we used to.

That's when it hits me. I know what we should do.

COLE

"I can't believe you remembered this place." She stands with her hands on her hips at the edge of the lake, smiling from ear to ear, eyes sparkling. Eyes as blue as the sky. I could stare into them all day, especially when she's as happy as she is now.

"You mean you forgot all the times we spent here?" I spread a blanket out on the grass and go back to the trunk to pull out the basket she packed.

"How could I forget that?" She's blushing a little when I get back to where she's waiting, and I don't think it's because of the slight chill in the breeze coming off the water. "You're the first person I ever went skinny dipping with."

"The first and only?" I ask, cocking one eyebrow.

"Uh, no. Just the first." She smirks as she sits cross-legged on the blanket. "Nice try, though."

I move so fast she gasps when she lands on her back with me on top of her. The sunlight shines into her eyes making them appear like sparkling gemstones. "Why do you like to lie to me?"

She blinks. "I was just teasing you. Why were you jealous?" she taunts.

"I pretended to myself I wasn't whenever I saw you linked to another man in some celebrity magazine or other, but fuck, Taylor, I'm insanely jealous. Hearing about you with any other guy makes my guts burn like acid."

She licks her lips. "What about you? Did you ... er ... bring anyone else here?"

"What do you think?"

She smiles cheekily. "No?"

"Go straight to the top of the class, Taylor Rose McCarthy."

Her smile becomes a grin. "You're turning me on. Either get off me or inside me."

"You'll pay for that later."

"What? Like the last time you said that."

The memory throws me off guard. That was the night I tied her up and teased her for hours without letting her come. She winks up at me and pushes me off her before turning back to unpacking the food. I lie back on the grass, hard as a rock, and watch her. How can she think about food after reminding me of that night? Now I'm remembering the moonlit nights when it was just the two of us, and all the times I took her right here in the grass. Or in the water. Or anywhere.

"Do you remember that night the grizzly came?" she asks.

Her expression makes me laugh.

"How can you laugh about that?" she shrieks. "I was scared to death. I thought it was going to tear us to pieces!"

"It wouldn't have because it wasn't a damn bear in the first place, but I'm sure the sound of you screaming and running around would've really protected us if that stray dog had been a bear."

"Stop calling it a dog. If it was a dog, it was a very big dog. Like abnormally big."

I lie back on my hands and laugh at the memory of that night.

She savagely tears at a baguette and layers cheese and sliced apple on top, then takes a big bite. "God, you're such a jerk."

"I'm just saying, you might have overreacted a little. That's all." I wonder if she knows how gorgeous she is when she's all fired up the way she is right now.

"Not half as much as you overreacted when you thought there were leeches in the lake. I can't even believe you would make fun of me when you're the one who ran out of the water, slapping at yourself, jumping around like the soles of your feet were on fire." She jumps to her feet and does an imitation which, I have to admit, is probably pretty accurate.

I crack open my ale with a laugh. "Because you're the one who said there were leeches out there!"

"I didn't say there were leeches on you," she points out between bursts of infectious giggles. "I only said I heard there were leeches in the lake and one of them attached itself to Jimmy Dolan's penis. That's all I said."

"You don't say a thing like that to a guy and expect him not to react the way I did. Certain things are precious," I say, taking the makeshift sandwich she hands me.

"Like the almighty penis," she says with a dramatic eye roll.

"Excuse me, Miss, but you weren't complaining about my almighty penis last night. All four times."

"No, but I doubt a simple little leech would've done much to hurt something as big as your dick." She winks at me again. Damn, does she have any idea what it does to me when she winks and gives me that sexy half-smile?

"Way to bring it back around," I chuckle as I tear into my sandwich and finish off my ale. There's something about being here with her, and it's not just the almost perfect weather. A little warmer and I might ask her to revisit our skinny-dipping days, only a lot more X-rated than before. I never used to understand when adults told me that youth was wasted on the young, but now I get it. When we were young and carefree, we didn't know shit about how to really have fun.

When the bread and toppings are gone and she's finished off her ale, Taylor stretches out on her back with one arm bent under her head. "I missed this. Isn't it funny how you can miss something and not know you're missing it until it's back in your life again? Then you look back, and you think, oh. That's what was wrong."

I stretch out, too, on my side so I can watch her. Clouds are starting to build; big, fluffy, white clouds that I watch passing overhead in the reflection in her eyes. Her hair is a puddle of gold under her head, sparkling against the blanket. She's so young and so impossibly gorgeous, but there's something in her that won't let her be happy. A grave maturity behind her perfect face. She's already lived an entire lifetime in the eight years we spent apart.

"You know you could have this again if you wanted it." What am I saying? Why can't I control the thoughts pouring out of my mouth? Why not give her my Letterman jacket while I'm at it and ask her if she wants to go steady? That's about the level of pushiness I'm exhibiting.

Her eyes shift until she's looking at me again. "Sorry, Cole, but you're going to have to work much harder than that to undo the past. It's not the sort of change that can happen overnight."

"I know. That doesn't mean I'm going to stop trying to keep you in my life by any means necessary."

"Oh?" She arches an eyebrow. "What do you plan to do? Tie me up and lock me away?"

"Don't give me any ideas." I lean over her and see her smile before my mouth is on hers and she's in my arms again.

"What happens if a bear comes along?" she murmurs between kisses, while her fingers dance over the back of my neck and across my shoulders.

"I guess we'll have to take our chances."

COLE

She can't stop looking at me. I can't stop looking at her. The light hanging over our table is like a spotlight shining on her, making her beauty stand out even stronger than ever. The porcelain skin, the sapphire eyes, the spun-gold hair.

My hands itch to bury themselves in that thick hair, the way they were buried earlier in the day. Thoughts of our picnic and what came after and everything leading up to it swirl around in my head. I know it's reflected in the way I'm looking at her, and I don't care. I don't care if everybody watching us sees my face and knows there's something going on.

She notices, too, and giggles. "If we're not careful, every-body's going to know what we've been up to," she whispers.

"Let them. They'll all be as envious of me as I would be if I saw you with anyone else."

She steals one of my cheese scones in retaliation. "Be careful what you wish for," she warns with a cryptic smile. "You'll find yourself all over the internet tomorrow as my new boyfriend."

"What would be so bad about that?" I wonder.

"Cole …"

"I know. I know. Fame isn't as fun as it looks." I don't want to downplay what she's going through. I really don't. I just hate seeing her in this fatalistic mood. I want to see the spark of joy in her eyes, and not just when we're naked, either.

Sure enough, there are people looking at us. She's not completely paranoid. I can imagine it would get old, fast, not being able to scratch my ass without a picture showing up on somebody's Instagram feed. I look at her cutting into a juicy piece of fried chicken and slipping it into her mouth. I love watching her eat. She is way too thin for my taste. I prefer her with more flesh on her bones.

"If you were so against being seen, why did you want to have dinner with me in public?"

She grins. "It's either this, or lasagna, blueberry muffins, or my cooking. Trust me you don't want to test my cooking skills."

"Are you that bad?"

"Is burning a bowl of cereal bad? If so, yes. Yes, I am."

I almost choke on a mouthful of chips. "You burned a bowl of cereal? How?"

She shakes her head. "Oh, Cole, Cole. You should know by now that with me, nothing is impossible."

We both laugh. "Yeah, but cereal doesn't need cooking."

She smiles. "I was eating out of a plastic bowl and put the bowl down on the stove when my phone rang…"

"Ah, but that doesn't count as cooking."

"There are other sorry tales that I won't go into if you don't mind," she says with a sheepish smile. "I guess my culinary skills extend to cooking a package of Ramen noodles, and that's only if I'm feeling saucy."

I lean back. I like her like this. "I guess you don't need to cook. You have people to do it for you."

She rolls her eyes. "True, but it's refreshing to live a semi-normal life sometimes."

"The way we common folk do?"

She snorts. "You've never been common, and you know it. You're a bit of a celebrity around these parts, aren't you?"

"I know how to cook a steak and I can eat a bowl of cereal without melting the bowl."

"I'll be sure to nominate you for a culinary genius award when I get a chance."

"You're so supportive." I turn my attention to my food. It tastes better than any other time I've been here. I don't know what it is about her, but she has a way of making everything better, no matter what we are doing.

"I think I got a little too much sun today." She puts a hand to her forehead, then picks up her beer and touches the cold glass to her skin instead. "I feel sort of drained, you know?"

"Could be all the activity we've been up to," I suggest with a knowing smile.

"You're good, but you're not that good."

"That's not what you were saying down at the lake."

"Yeah, well, you're not good enough to suck the life force out of me. No offense. I hope that doesn't hurt your ego."

"I'm a big boy. I can take it." I look at her with fresh eyes. Have I been careless with her health? She does look a little flushed. I frown. "You do look a little off."

"Oh, thanks," she says with a smirk.

"You women. You'll never let a man win."

She rolls her eyes. "A tired argument."

"I mean it! You say you don't feel well. I agree and you get mad at me. I bet if I told you that you look great and it doesn't seem like there's anything wrong, you would accuse me of ignoring the way you feel, or play it down, something like that. There's no winning."

"Anyway, we should go. You probably just need some rest. I've been keeping you up."

"Oh." Her face falls. "I was hoping you would keep me up again tonight."

Something stirs inside me. I look at the hectic color in her cheeks. "We'll see how you feel when we get to the house."

COLE

An hour later, we're sitting on the couch with a movie playing on the TV. She's curled up next to me, her head on my lap, bundled up under a handmade blanket. I'm stroking the top of her head and wondering how something so simple could feel so good. Her hair smells of apples. I could stroke it forever. I don't even know what we're watching, but it doesn't matter. We're having too much fun picking it apart.

"Oh, my God. Somebody got paid to write this crap?" she giggles.

"Hey. At least everybody is pretty. Pretty people don't have to say things that make actual sense."

She giggles again. "I do like the costumes."

"Yeah, they're okay."

"Except nobody who's supposedly poor would wear something that fancy."

"Oh, you're a costume expert now, too?"

"I have my interests."

She goes back to paying attention to the movie, and I go back to stroking her hair. She lets out a satisfied little sigh and moves around like a cat, stretching and wriggling to get more comfortable.

It shouldn't happen, but it does. I wonder how many other men have been in this position with her. Something so innocent, but it wouldn't seem so innocent when it was anybody but me. I imagine that jerk-off from last night. Was he ever the guy sitting with her head in his lap, watching a movie and touching her hair? Did he guide her head to other places in his lap?

Did she go? Did she give in to what he wanted? No. I take a deep breath and tell myself to chill out. He's nobody to be jealous of. None of the other men in her life are worth being jealous of. If there are any. I know her. I've known her since she was six years old. Fame might change people, but I can't believe it changes their basic nature. It's not in her nature to be that way. She still has that veneer of innocence, like there's a shell around her and none of the bad shit can get through.

Even so, my hand tightens into a claw, and she notices.

"What's wrong?" She pushes herself up on her forearms and twists a little so she can look me in the eye. "Are you okay?"

Her eyes are so wide and innocent. It's like she's staring into my soul when she looks at me the way she is. I hate the thoughts I was having. I hate doubting her, wondering what kind of person she is. She doesn't deserve it. "Yeah, I'm fine." I smooth the hair back from her face and tuck a strand behind her ear. "You okay? Feeling any better?"

"I think so. I just needed this. You know. Time to relax and just be." She sits up and leans on my arm. "I'm glad it's with you."

"Yeah?"

"You're the only one I could ever do this with," she murmurs with her head against my shoulder. "You think I've ever been able to sit down and watch a movie and make snarky comments about it? It's not much fun when you're talking to yourself."

"No other movie buffs in your life?" I can't help myself from fishing.

"No. And you know it. Smartass." She shakes her head with a wry smile and goes back to watching the movie. So do I. It's enough for now. What we have right now, right here at this moment, is enough.

Then she climbs into my lap, facing me, and winds her arms around my neck. This is better. I rest my hands on her hips, only a thin pair of yoga pants between my skin and hers. She presses her body against mine.

"What about the movie?" I murmur as our mouths brush tantalizingly against each other once, twice.

"What about it?" Her tongue darts over my lips and I groan. "I've already seen it—besides, you're much, much more interesting." She rolls her hips in circles over my crotch and I'm hard in an instant, aching for her. She smiles when she feels me growing, and rubs her pussy harder against me. I slide my hands up over her sides, taking her t-shirt with me, and she lets go of me just long enough to raise her arms over her head so I can take it off.

She raises herself off my lap, breaking the precious contact, to present me with her breasts. I slide my tongue in circles over her nipples until they tighten into peaks, then suck them one after the other. She moans my name, running her fingers through my hair, tangling it, pulling it, and sending bolts of lightning from her fingertips to my dick.

I need more of her.

My mouth takes inventory of her soft skin, her sweet scent. I lower her to the cushions and trail slow, wet kisses down her flat stomach, down to the waistband of her pants. Her hips are rolling the way they were when she was in my lap. I hear her panting and whimpering, whispering that she needs me, that she wants more. I slide my fingers under the waistband and pull the pants over her hips, down her thighs, until her lean legs are bare. She parts them, and I run my hands from ankle to hip, loving how exceptionally soft and smooth her skin is.

"Take me," she whispers, looking up at me with half-lidded eyes.

I lower my head until it's between her legs and her scent is all around me, pulling me in, drawing me closer. Fuck it. My mouth is watering. I have to taste.

"Mmm ... yes ..." She arches her back and holds my head in place with both hands as I slide my tongue over her slick cleft before going deeper. She moans and writhes, and her body is like a wave, undulating beneath me until I have to hold her still so I can pleasure her. When she comes, her cries fill the room and her thighs squeeze me like a vice.

I drive myself into her. She wraps her arms and legs around me and holds me tight, making me wonder where I end and she begins. I go deep, as deep as I can, letting her ride me as I ride her. Our bodies work together, moving in sync, building up to something bigger than the two of us. When we come, we come together, gasping and grunting and gripping each other like our lives depend on it. Maybe they do.

"I don't know how it's going to work out for us either, but I want to try again. With you," she whispers.

I feel so happy it feels as if my heart will burst. This is all my dreams, my birthdays, all my Christmases wrapped up in one perfect moment.

TAYLOR

I've spent the night in his arms. The whole night with Cole wrapped around me, holding me close, protecting me from anything that might come along. Now, I hear him walking around the bedroom. I lie still, eyes closed. I'm in that sweet spot between being asleep and awake, just drifting along. I don't want to leave it. Real life has been sweet lately —very sweet—but this dream where I'm married to Cole is even sweeter.

I feel young again. I really do. I'm happy. I feel happy and light and I am so incredibly glad to be alive. There is nobody here who wants to take advantage of me. I want to savor the moment.

I wonder what he's doing. He's trying to be sneaky. He always was a sneak. He'd buy me presents and pretend that we just came upon them in the woods. I still have that pretty love heart locket that we just happened to find under a fallen leaf. Maybe he wants to surprise me. The thought makes me smile, which of course gives away that I'm awake.

He sits on the edge of the bed, close to me. I open my eyes and my smile dies. He is fully dressed. I start to feel sick. I didn't expect him to leave so soon, with no fanfare. There I was, thinking he wanted to make me happy. Stupid Taylor. You should've known better. "Where are you going? Are you leaving?"

His beautiful eyes sweep over my face, reading me like a book. "I'm not leaving. I'm just going to town for a minute." He strokes my cheek with his fingertips, then cups my chin in his palm. "You have to learn to trust me, Taylor. I'm not leaving. Ever. This is it for you. You are stuck with me forever."

I shrug, speechless for a minute.

"Didn't I tell you I won't let you go this time? Did you think I was lying?"

Oh, right. I forgot about that. "I guess … I don't know … it's hard for me to believe something like that."

"Oh, sweet Taylor, when will I gain your trust again?" He leans down to kiss me and I let myself sink into the kiss. His lips are warm and tender, but possessive. He has the strength I've been missing for so long. I want to let him take care of me. I want to give myself to him because I know he'll never take advantage of me. He's the only man who never took advantage of me. He's my safe place. I wrap a hand around the back of his neck and start pulling him down on top of me, but he pulls back.

"Hey, I have plans for us." He touches his forehead to mine and smiles.

"Oh. Right." I sit up then, running my hands through my hair.

It's a mess. He doesn't seem to care, plus, he's the one who made it that way. "So? Where are you going?"

"I thought I'd pick up some breakfast since I can't trust you to fix us anything."

I laugh. "What's wrong with you? Is steak the only thing you know how to cook?"

"No comment," he chuckles. "Maybe you're not the only one who never had to learn how to cook."

"I thought so," I say with a smile. "Okay. What's for breakfast, then?"

"I was thinking … fresh fried apple muffins. What do you think?" Like he has to ask. My eyes go round and my mouth starts watering. I'm like Pavlov's dog. I can't believe he remembers my obsession with fried apple muffins. Not just any sort of muffins, either. Like those plastic-wrapped pieces of garbage they sell at gas stations. These are baked fresh at Sharon's Bakery.

"You remember," I whisper with a smile.

"How could I forget? You've made me go out of my way to find them more times than I can count."

"I know."

"You wanted to develop an app—"

"Yes, Cole. I get it. You remember because I have a fried apple muffin problem." I shove him playfully and he laughs.

"I thought it would be a nice gesture," he says with a smile that makes his dimples stand out. It is almost shy, a thing one could associate with a man's man like him. I can't tease him anymore when he smiles like that. Even though I know he's playing around. Trying to melt me. Which he's doing, and very well, but still.

"It would be. I'm starving. Why are you still sitting here?"

"That's because you were trying to get in my pants, like, twenty seconds ago."

"That was before you put the thought of fried apple muffins in my head. Go! Get moving!" I try to shove him off the bed, but his feet are so solidly planted on the floor. It's like trying to move a wall. He doesn't budge an inch. Laughing my head off I start using my feet instead.

"Fine, fine!" He gets up and he's laughing, too, and I think *this* is it. This is what I want, forever. Laughing with him over stupid things, being silly, teasing each other and looking forward to spending the morning together. My heart has never felt so full.

TAYLOR

I wait until I hear the front door close before I jump out of bed and hurry to the bathroom for a shower. I can't believe it: I miss him already. I giggle to myself just thinking about him coming back with the muffins and the idea of hanging out with him all day. It's crazy, the way he's so deep in me, like he's formed roots that have wound their way all through my soul.

As I wash, I remember the feeling of Cole's hands on me. The way his tongue drove me crazy. The way his body moved along mine, inside me and above me and all over me, everywhere.

I need to hurry up and finish showering, which means I need to stop thinking about him or else I'll end up with pruny skin and no more hot water. I wash my hair, condition it, rinse it off, and hop out of the tub.

The room is full of steam. I wipe it off the mirror and look at myself, really look at myself for the first time since I came back to town. Who is this girl? She has sparkling eyes and color in her cheeks, color that isn't just from the hot shower. She's smiling, too, and it's not for a camera or her screaming fans. She's smiling because she's really, genuinely happy. So much that she could just about burst from it.

With a big grin I turn away from the mirror and grab a towel. It's a far cry from the luxurious pile I'm used to, but I hum to myself as I dry off, which turns into singing. When's the last time I randomly burst into song? Usually, I have to be careful of overusing my voice in between appearances. I don't care very much about that right now.

Music is just bursting to come out of my skin. I sing some of the songs I performed with Cole back at Artie's and start to think that Cole could be right about me performing where and when I feel like it. Sure, I won't be the superstar I am now, but the real truth about that is been there got the T-shirt, had enough.

Singing the songs I want to sing and doing what makes me happy is what I want now. I want to concentrate on the sort of music that makes me want to perform. Not the mindless jingles that sells by the millions. I want to be in control of my life. What else is there if not? To run on a hamster wheel for the rest of my life?

I switch on the hairdryer and marvel at how much my outlook has changed in almost no time. All because of him. I've told myself time and again over the years that I can't and won't rely on a man to make me happy. Nobody but I can do that. I've sworn to myself that I'll never, ever let a man's opinion steer my actions. I rely on my instincts. I know myself best, after all. Yet here I am, happily letting his ideas into my brain. But it feels like a good thing. It's all so good.

How have I gone around without him for so long? What was I thinking?

The ringing of the doorbell makes me laugh. No way he could've gotten to town, waited at the bakery, and come back that quickly. I throw my wet hair into a messy bun as I run down the stairs. "Forget your wallet?" I call out, laughing, as I throw open the door.

It's not him though. I never thought it might not be him.

"Victoria?" I spit the name out like it's poison, because it is. I haven't seen her since high school and would've died happy if I never saw her again. Ugh, why did she have to catch me without make-up, wearing grungy clothes, and my hair still wet? Anyway, why do I even care?

I guess no matter how much money I make, no matter how many fans I have all over the world—not to mention the people I hang out with, who probably wouldn't look twice at her since she's nothing but a big fish in a small pond—I'm still reduced to the poor, somewhat outcast kid who happens to be able to sing. Just the way it was when we were kids.

She doesn't bother with pleasantries. "We need to talk."

"What about?" I don't move to allow her into the house. She stands on the porch, looking like a million bucks. Some people don't have to be flashy about their wealth. You can just tell they're wealthy by the way they carry themselves, the way they wear even simple clothes. I used to worry I'll never get to that point. That I'll never wear my hair just the right way, or wear the wrong clothes because I wasn't raised with money. Not like Victoria.

"We have things to discuss." I can't see her eyes behind her big, dark glasses, but her tone of voice is more than enough to tell me she still looks down on me. Maybe more than ever before, which is saying something since she always treated me like the shit that got stuck to the bottom of her shoe.

I lift my chin. "I can't imagine that we have anything to discuss, Victoria. We didn't ten years ago, and we certainly don't now."

"I think we do. The talk is all over town that Cole's car was parked outside your house overnight."

"What the hell has it got to do with you?"

"Let me in, or we'll have this out in the middle of the street. I'm sure the media will enjoy getting a hold of that story."

"Oh for crying out loud, just get in." I step aside and hold the door open so she can come in. Surprisingly, I manage not to slam the door once she's inside. She slides her glasses to the top of her head and looks around like she knows people lived this way, but has never seen it with her own eyes.

A shiver of rage runs up my spine, and I wish to God I could give into it. I'd love to tear out her smooth, thick, perfectly highlighted hair. I clear my throat sarcastically.

She stops going over the furniture and pictures and faces me, instead. "Sorry to burst in on your morning."

"Why pretend? You're not sorry."

"You're right. I'm not," she admits coolly.

"What are you doing here, Victoria?"

"You can't imagine how disappointed I was when I found out you've been shacking up here with Cole."

"Shacking up? I'd hardly call spending a couple of days with my own boyfriend 'shacking up,' so watch your language."

"Your boyfriend?" she sneers. "Honey, he was your boyfriend eight years ago. He's my fiancé now." She sweeps her long, chocolate brown hair over one shoulder and holds up her left hand. On it is a diamond that could choke a horse. "Guess who gave me this?"

The shock of her claim makes me stagger. There's a girl in front of me who is wearing a diamond that might have come from him. My head starts to reel. It's not possible. It can't be. No way. But why would she arrive on my front porch if it wasn't true? Why would she be here, pursing her lips the way they're pursed, popping out one hip like she's daring me to start a fight? Humiliation and dread and complete disgust start to creep all through me.

She rolls her big, dark eyes. "You're not going to faint on me, are you?"

I want to be strong in front of her, but it's hard. Really hard when my whole life is being turned upside down. I cross my arms over my chest like a protective shield. "You're lying," I whisper.

"Why would I lie? You left eight years ago. What did you think, that Cole would wait for you like a monk? I'm sorry to tell you, but you've been sleeping with my fiancé, Taylor."

I can't help it. No matter how hard I fight against letting her see me react, I reel back like she slapped me. No. It's not possible. For God's sake, why does it have to be her? Of all the women in the entire world, why her? Cole knows how much I detest her. I can't remember all the times she's put me down, made me feel lower than dirt because I didn't hit the paternity jackpot the way she did. Just because her father owns the other half of the town that Cole's father doesn't, she's treated like royalty. She acts like she is, too.

"Your fiancé?" I echo. Even seeing the ring didn't hit home as hearing her call him that.

"Yeah. Fiancé. As in engaged to be married."

"Since when?"

She places her sunglasses on the coffee table and runs a hand through her hair, shaking it out like a chocolate waterfall. As I stare at it in a daze, I pick up the scent of her shampoo and smoothing serum. I feel sick when I think of him burying his nose in my hair and telling me he missed the smell of my shampoo.

"For ages now," she says, a cruel tilt to her cultured voice. "I mean, it's always been assumed that we would get married. We come from the same background and we get on. We just had to make it official, which we did … a year ago."

She loves this. I can almost taste the satisfaction pouring out of her. Like spending kindergarten through junior year making my life miserable wasn't enough. She needs to spike the ball in the end zone. Ever since I can remember she has always had it in for me. Why does she hate me so much? I never did a thing to her. It's like she decided from the first day of school that my misery would be her lifelong, personal project. So she stands there, blithe and calm and crushes my heart under her designer shoes.

I won't let myself crumble to pieces in front of her. "He's never spoken a word about you," I say. At least my voice is a little stronger than before.

"I find that hard to believe—but I guess it makes sense in a way. He wanted to slum it for a few days."

"How dare you," I hiss.

"I dare because that's exactly what he was doing, and if you're honest, you won't deny it either." She waves her hands around the living room. "I mean, come on. Do you think this is anything like what he's used to?"

"It's not even what I'm used to anymore," I cry defensively. "I only came back for the funeral."

She folds her arms, mimicking my pose. Only she looks better doing it, an Amazon wearing all-black except for a khaki trench coat. "Please. We both know that this is the real you. Everything else is just what you picked up. You can put all the lipstick you want on a pig, but they're still a pig."

"Go to hell," I snap. "And get your head out of your ass while you're there. I don't know who died and made you Queen, but I'm waiting to hear Cole's side of this."

She shakes her head mournfully. "It's always the same with people like you. You earn a little money, get a little famous, and you think it makes you a decent person. You will always be the girl who grew up poor. And one day, everything will come crashing down on you. Probably because you'll do something to screw it all up, the way people who secretly know they're no good always do. Cole's too good for you, and you know it. He might have forgotten it, but he'll remember. He's just a man. Sometimes they don't think too clearly when they're using their other head. Know what I mean?"

I'm about ready to projectile vomit all over her designer clothes. This bitch. I straighten my spine. "Where do you get off judging me? Are you so bored that you need to go around tearing other people down? Maybe you need a hobby?"

"No, sweetheart. I need you to leave my fiancé alone. That's what I need. My fiancé …" She pauses for effect. "The father of my baby."

TAYLOR

My legs fold up, and I land on the sofa with a thud. The sofa where we just made love last night.

"A baby." I wish I could come up with something more intelligent, but she has me at a loss. A big, fat, major loss.

She covers her stomach with her hands. "Yes, I'm pregnant. And no, I didn't trap him. It was an accident, but he was more than happy for us to keep it. After all we had already decided to get married by then. You need to step aside and let the rest of us get back to living our lives. You had your chance years ago and you blew it. Maybe you even had a bit of fun here with him, but it's over now."

I can't even look at her. I was sleeping with her fiancé. Her baby's father. I'm the bad guy. I force myself to look up. "He never said a word about it. That's the truth."

She shrugs like it doesn't matter. "I'm willing to let it go, because the two of you did mean something to each other back in the day. I guess having you back in town made him go a little crazy. Nostalgia, you know. I'm trying to be the bigger person, but I've got my baby's happiness to think of. You wouldn't want to be a home wrecker, would you?"

I don't understand. I feel so confused. How could Cole be the way he was with me if he had a fiancée? Why didn't he tell me? How could he? How could I have so completely misjudged him? Are they on a break? Did they break-up and she can't come to terms with it? I realize I'm making excuses for him, but I need to do something. Anything to stop the pain in my chest from spreading. I can't believe he would lie to me like that.

"Are you two happy?" I search her face for any sign of a reaction, anything that will tell me she's lying.

"We're very much in love," she says with a slow, satisfied smile. "We have been for years. We got together at my niece's christening party three years ... after you left." The last three words are a reproach, a curse. She perches on the edge of the opposite sofa, like she doesn't want to let her clothes touch it.

She sighs, rubbing her hands together. The diamond gleams and shines and sparkles. "I won't lie to you. He was pretty broken up about you leaving. I guess—I don't know—the romances we have when we're young affect us more strongly. I'll give him that much. I was there for him even before we started going out together. What I'm saying is I picked up the pieces. I made sure he didn't do anything rash, which he might have done. For a while it was bad. And that was when we got closer, but after the party we knew what he had with you was the lust of a hormonal boy and what we had was the real thing. Neither of us has looked back since then."

"Except for now. When I came to town," I say slowly.

"Except for that." Her lips tighten. "I don't know—maybe he wanted to get you out of his system, once and for all. That makes perfect sense to me. Look at it this way. You can finally have him out of your system, too. Right?" The way she says it, it sounds like she's doing me a favor. Like I should be thanking her.

"I guess so," I hear myself whisper, my mind going around in circles. He wanted us to be together. I know I'm not wrong about that. Maybe he really does, but like a leopard never changes its spots, he hasn't altered either. Despite all his protestations that he was a kid then and he is a man now, he is still the same unreliable person he was years ago. Then he changed his mind at the last minute and left me in the lurch, and now it looks like he is doing the same thing to Victoria. I can't stand Victoria, but good luck to her. Let her have him. I don't want a man who is so fickle and changeable. I want a man who is an unshakeable rock. A man who keeps his promises. Cole has broken every promise he ever made to me.

"Hey," Victoria adds, "your life isn't even here anymore. This town? You've outgrown it. Right?" She raises an eyebrow. "Listen. I was pissed off and hurt before, and I said some things I shouldn't have said. About you being trashy, I mean. I won't pretend like I've never followed your career. Maybe it's morbid fascination, I don't know. Or I might have wanted to keep tabs on the girl my boyfriend, now fiancé, used to love. Who knows? Regardless, you've done well for yourself. Really. You should be proud."

"Thank you." In over twenty years she has never been nice to me. Any compliments were backhanded, and came with caveats. Once another friend of mine said that her compliments were like cupcakes with shards of broken glass inside them. They're not completely complimentary. Right now, compared to the way things normally are between us, we're practically best friends.

"You don't belong here anymore. I mean, nothing changes here. You're jet-setting around the world, while half the people in this sleepy little ghost town don't know how to use Facebook. Don't waste your time dredging up the past. It won't get you anywhere."

"You're right about that," I admit, strange as it sounds coming out of my mouth. I don't belong here. I should leave and have an agent take care of the house for me, right down to the packing. Hell, I actually don't want anything from this house anyway. I don't want anything to do with it, or this town, or Cole, ever again. It was all a mistake, a waste of time. Who would have guessed Victoria of all people would steer me straight?

"Cole won't be coming back," she says, standing and going to the door. "I'll take care of that. You take care of the rest of your life and leave the rest of us to our lives. Okay?"

"Yeah. Sure."

"Because if you don't, I'll make sure the entire world knows you've been screwing the father of my child."

Ah, there's the girl I know. She couldn't let it go at that. She had to twist the knife in my chest. I don't even look at her. I can't. I'm staring at the floor, and that's as far up as my eyes will go. If I look at her, I'll have to claw her eyes out.

"I get it. Just go." I want to see her to the door. I would still love to kick her ass, pregnant or not, but I can't move. I'm like a block of ice. The sound of the door closing is more like the sound of my dreams ending.

I fooled myself again.

TAYLOR

Minutes later I'm in the back seat of the rented car with the driver taking me back to the hotel. I waited all of thirty seconds after Victoria left before calling him to get me. I grabbed my bag and ran out the second the car arrived.

How could I have been so stupid?

I close my eyes to avoid looking at anything, any part of the town, or any of the people in it. It's all in the distant past. None of it matters anymore, if it ever did in the first place. I'm a bigger, better person now. I should've known better than to let myself get sucked back in the way I did. What a mistake. What a terrible, awful, stupid mistake.

And him! He's the greatest disappointment of my life.

No, I can't think about him right now. I need to get through the car ride. Then I need to get through the hotel. I'll be there only as long as it'll take to schedule a flight out of town. Because I need to get out of here. I need to get back home. Once I'm home, I'll let go. I'll cry my heart out then.

This isn't home. This is hell.

I rest my head against the seat and cover my face with my hands. How? How did I leave myself open to getting hurt like this? I'm supposed to be a smart person. For God's sake, I was just thinking earlier about how I'd promised myself that I wouldn't let a man dictate my life or make decisions for me. There I was, before Victoria showed up with her news, telling myself it would be okay to let Cole back into my life. To think I was so happy this morning when he told me he wasn't going to leave for good. He wanted us to be together. What a sucker I am.

I fight back the bile that rises in my throat. It's a good thing I never ate, or else I would lose it right now, all over the back seat of the car. Oh, it hurts. It hurts so much. My whole body is wracked with pain, actual pain, something physical that feels like it's tearing me apart.

I can't stop thinking about him, even though I've told myself not to. I keep seeing his eyes. His smile. I hear his voice and feel the pressure of his fingers on my cheek when he asks if I don't know him well enough by now to know he wouldn't sneak out on me. Damn me for believing him. Either he's the world's greatest actor, or I'm the most naïve fool on earth. He was believable, right down to the way his voice trembled a little when he said he didn't want us ever to be apart again. The only explanation I can come up with is he believed himself. Just like he ran out on me, he must have planned to run out on her.

A tear slides down my cheek, and I brush it away distractedly. I don't deserve the relief of tears. How stupid do you have to be to fall for the same shit all over again? *Fool me once, shame on you, fool me twice, shame on me.*

"You're such an idiot," I whisper, turning my head to look out the window and gauge how far we are from the hotel. Only a couple of minutes more. We're already just around our exit. I'm so glad I decided to take a room so far outside of town. I don't have to run the risk of bumping into him before I go.

"Here we are." The driver pulls up out front of the ivy covered entrance. I shove what's fallen out of my half-open bag back inside before getting out. I look down at my clothes and smooth them down. There will be people at the hotel. It's bad enough I look like I just rolled out of bed since I couldn't waste a minute and take the chance of running into him. I still have to consider my image. Actually, it is all I have left.

I hurry through the lobby and fish through my bag for the key to my room. Thank God I took it with me and didn't leave it with reception. The last thing I want is to talk to anyone.

I nod at the receptionist, who looks at me with bright eyes, and quickly walk up the carpeted stairs. I open the door and lean against it. The suite looks strange, yet familiar. I should've stayed here. No, even better. I should've left after the funeral. I should've gone straight back. Why on earth did I stay? Why? Why? Why did I allow him back into my heart?

I could so easily have avoided all this.

I dial up my assistant. "Yeah, it's me." I drop my carry-on and go to the closet where the rest of my clothes are stored. I pull out my suitcase and get to work throwing everything inside. "I need you to book me the first flight out of here. I don't care when it is. Just get me a flight."

"What's the matter?" Her voice sounds anxious. I guess I'd be anxious, too, if my normally level-headed boss lost her mind all of a sudden.

"Nothing. Nothing major, anyway. I just need to get out of here. I've stayed too long. It wasn't a good idea."

"Oh, I'm sorry." I hear tapping in the background and assume it means she's on her laptop. I check the time. It's barely nine in the morning, which means it's even earlier for her. I know lots of people in my position who don't give a damn either way. They'll wake up their team at any time, day or night, for the slightest things. On a whim, sometimes. And they never apologize. They don't even think about giving a bonus, or something for the extra work. Me, on the other hand? I'm already planning a way to say thank you that is worth more than words.

"Okay," she says. "I can get you out on United in two hours. Is that enough time?"

"More than enough," I say, zipping up my suitcase. "Thank you for going out of your way this morning, Rachael. I really appreciate it."

"Don't sweat it. What about security?"

"I won't need it. I'm travelling incognito. No one will recognize me."

"Are you sure?"

"It's a small airport and I'll be fine," I reassure.

"Do you want me to meet you at the airport over at this end?"

"No, I don't think so. I'll just go straight home. I could use the rest of the day to myself, but come by tomorrow."

"Will do. The confirmation email and ticket should come through in a minute or two. Have a good flight."

TAYLOR

I hang up. My hands are shaking. I'll be home soon. Everything will make sense there. Maybe I'll spend the rest of the day in bed, under the covers. Maybe I'll watch a movie and zone out. No, that will just remind me of last night. I hate myself now for making it so easy for him, for throwing myself at him the way I did.

I collapse onto the bed, still shaking, only now I'm shaking from head to toe, almost violently. I made it so easy. I threw myself at him. I trusted him, stupid as it was. I thought I could give him my heart and trust him with it.

Tears start to flow, and I let them for a few minutes. I know I need to get to the airport. Usually Rachael will call ahead and warn the airport authorities that I'm flying and I don't exactly have to follow the rules when it comes to waiting in line for security checks. One of the perks of being a star.

Instead of getting out of bed and going back down to the lobby, I take a pillow and hold it to myself. Pretty soon I'm sobbing. Great, huge, breathless sobs that seem to come up from my toes and travel all through my body. I'm not just crying for what happened today. I'm crying for that day at the audition, the way he betrayed me. I'm crying for all the times since then that he still lived in my heart. I'm crying because I wanted so, so, so much to believe that he loved me.

He's so cruel. Showing me what it might feel like to be loved, then taking it all away like that. Making me remember what it felt like to perform and be happy about it. Telling me that I don't have to be unhappy. Even giving me advice. The sadistic bastard.

I punch the pillow with one fist even as I hold it tight with my other arm. Pretty soon I'm on my knees with the pillow on the bed and I'm pounding it with both fists, raising my arms straight up and slamming them down. Grunting and screaming each time I land a blow.

Oh, God. I'm losing it. I'm losing my mind. I collapse, exhausted, soaked with tears. I feel empty inside, totally hollowed out.

I need to get out of here as soon as possible. I don't ever want to lay eyes on him again. I know one thing for sure: I'll never let Cole betray me again. It was natural, wanting to give him another chance after he left me hanging at the audition. I gave him a second chance, but I don't believe in third chances.

I better get ready for the airport, which means I need to look semi-presentable so I don't call attention to myself. I slide from the bed and stumble to the bathroom. My legs feel like rubber. I splash cold water on my face, water so cold it stings like needles, but it helps. I wet a washcloth and hold it over my eyes for a minute in the hopes of calming down some of the swelling.

When I lower the washcloth and look at myself, the difference from earlier this morning is staggering. God, that wasn't even an hour ago. I was so happy. Oh, I was so perfectly happy. So happy, I sang for no reason other than pure joy. I had hope. I had trust in a man I loved, who I thought loved me back. I thought I had a future with him.

Look at me now. Hollow-eyed, haunted. I drag a brush through my hair and braid it over one shoulder, change out the sweats for a loose, cotton, dress before wrapping myself in an oversized cardigan that reaches halfway down my thighs. With boots and sunglasses, I don't look like Taylor Rose, the star anymore. Unless someone looks really close I'll be able to fly unrecognized. Nobody will be expecting me to travel on my own.

"We're going to the airport," I announce after calling the driver. "Immediately. I'm on my way down now."

"United," I tell him as he takes my bag and loads it into the trunk. I thought no one would notice me, but there are more than a few interested faces peering at me as I walk around to the open door and slide into the car. I think I hear the sound of a few phone cameras going off, too. I turn my head away and thank God for big sunglasses.

It reminds me of Victoria's glasses. She left them on the coffee table. It's almost enough to make me want to go back, just to crush them under my heel before flying home.

One hot, salty tear rolls down my cheek and I wipe it away. That's the last tear I'll shed for Cole or myself. It's time to harden my heart, because I can't get hurt like this again.

COLE

There are a lot of people waiting their turn, and now there is a woman who can't make up her mind whether she should get a doughnut, or a cupcake. For fuck's sake. It's not life and death. Just get both. I look at my watch impatiently.

I want to get back to Taylor.

Would anybody recognize me if they saw me acting like a pathetic love-sick fool? I doubt it. I'm the guy who swore off women a long time ago. Whenever I have an itch I get it scratched by one chick or another, usually from a neighboring town. Then, I move along. It's worked well enough for me.

Yes, sex with whatever piece of ass I picked up at the bar or the club was fine, but it has nothing on looking into Taylor's eyes and seeing what she feels while I'm inside her. Being able to let go of myself, all the pretenses and the masks I've learned to wear over the years? It's everything. She's everything.

"Is this a holiday or something?" someone mutters as he elbows his way to the counter. The bitter chuckling around me says I'm not the only one put-out by the wait.

The girl behind the counter makes eye contact and blushes before she looks away. I want to tell her she's barking up the wrong tree, but that might be a little harsh. I look out the window at Main Street, instead. I guess every small town has a street like this, full of storefronts. People walk back and forth, smiling at each other and asking about each other's business, but underneath the sugar coating is a lemon drop.

I'm too big for this place, and so is Taylor. It broke my heart, but I'm glad she left. She would've spent the rest of her life playing in places like Artie's, making next to nothing and feeling resentful. Singing would've become her side gig, what she did on the weekends while she worked in some going-nowhere job to make ends meet.

She has the kind of talent that needs an entire world to hold it.

A town like this would've squashed it, or put it out like a flickering flame. No matter how disappointed she is with fame, it's what she wanted. She's been dreaming of it since she was a little girl and she would have always wondered what would've happened if she gave it a try instead of playing small and staying out of the spotlight. Her soul would've withered down to nothing. I'm sure of it. No matter how unhappy she thinks she is now, it's nothing compared to how she'd feel otherwise.

"Number forty-seven!"

"That's me." I hold my ticket up and navigate through the crowd. There's a box of fresh muffins waiting for me on the counter. I know Taylor must be starving, since I've been waiting for almost an hour.

"They'd better be great," I say to the girl behind the counter.

"The best in town. Nice and moist."

"How many do you want?" The girl working behind the counter at the bakery is doing just about everything but licking her lips at me. I wonder what Taylor would think about that if she saw it. I have to bite the side of my tongue to keep from smiling and probably encouraging the kid.

"Give me four. No, six." I've seen Taylor eat three in a sitting. I wonder how much she must work out to keep her body as tight as it is.

After paying, I pick up the pink, string-tied box and make my way out. It's good to get a little fresh air once I step outside.

"Cole!" I turn to find a pair of girls walking down the street in my direction. I recognize them. They're servers at Artie's. "Is Taylor still in town?"

"Yeah, she's around." She would hate it if she knew I was talking about her, but they seem like harmless kids. Just genuine fans who had an exciting night when their favorite singer performed in the bar they worked at. What kind of excitement can they possibly get around here, anyway? I can't imagine things have picked up much since I was growing up.

"God, it was so much fun when you guys played together. I don't think we ever had such a good night. Last night was so boring by comparison. Everyone was saying the same thing and talking about you guys. Will you guys come back and play again?"

I laugh. "Yeah, well, I don't know. It was kind of a one-off."

"Oh please," one of them begs.

"Look, I can't promise anything. I'll let Taylor decide."

Their eyes light up. "You could always come in tonight. Why don't you come in tonight," one of them suggests, as if she just thought of it. I stifle a wry smile. The two of them are like clones who take cues from their favorite celebrities. I notice they're both wearing their hair the same way Taylor did when we visited the bar, pinned back in barrettes at the sides with soft waves framing their faces. Does this sort of thing happen to her all the time? She chooses a hairstyle and impressionable young girls copy her. That kind of hero worship must be heady.

"I don't know. I can't make any promises for Taylor."

One of them looks down at the box. "Ooh, what's in there? It smells amazing."

Which is my cue to get moving. I have a hungry woman at home. "Muffins." I wink conspiratorially. "They're for Taylor."

This little bit of information makes them lean against each other and squeal. "That is so sweet!"

Yeah, well, I'm a sweet guy. "See you around." I get in the car before they can ask any more questions.

COLE

It's not far back to her house, and thank God for that. I've already been away from her for too long. I think of what we should do today. We have to work out some plan of action that suits both of us, but I'm not spoiling today with reality. Real life will have to wait until tomorrow. Tomorrow is when I'll get it together. In all likelihood I'll move to LA and start a business there. I've been wanting to leave my father's business for a long time now and Taylor is the perfect excuse.

I'm whistling to myself as I jog up the front steps, then I remember at the last second that I locked the door behind me. I lean on the bell for a second and expect to hear her feet pounding down the stairs, starving for muffins. She's a fiend when it comes to fried apple muffins.

I don't hear her stomp down the stairs. I don't hear anything.

Maybe she's in the shower? I ring again, then knock a few times and call. Still nothing. I look around—the street's empty. No sign of her.

I call, knock again, and press my ear to the door. I don't hear a sound. It feels as if there is no one home.

"What the hell?" I mutter and move towards the window. It's locked, with the curtains only half-drawn. It's dark in there. There isn't even any light in the upstairs hall.

I pull out my phone to see if she called. She hasn't, and there aren't any texts. Dread blooms in my chest. What the hell game is she playing? No, not a game. She doesn't play games. There has to be a good reason. Thank God I had the presence of mind to exchange numbers with her last night. I call her number and wait, but there's no answer.

"Taylor, what's going on? I got here and you're gone. Tell me you're okay, please," I say into the answering machine. I hang up and pace back and forth a few times in front of her door, replaying everything from this morning. No, nothing happened between us that would make her leave. There's got to be something else.

I cup my hands around my eyes and lean in to peer through the window again. I have to wait a minute for my eyes to adjust to the almost nonexistent light. Slowly, the furniture starts to come into focus. I see the couch and the coffee table …

Wait. I squint to get a better look. There's a pair of sunglasses sitting on the table. I've never seen Taylor wear a pair like that, with the interlocking C's on the arms, up by the hinges. Chanel.

I do know somebody else who wears the exact same sunglasses.

I take a step back, away from the window. No. It's not possible. Why would she come here? Yeah, they could be some-body else's sunglasses, but there are very few women in this town who can afford to fly to New York for their sunglasses and it would be too big a coincidence for another Chanel-wearing woman to pay Taylor a visit while I was gone. Was she watching the house? Waiting for the moment when I was away? To do what?

"Are you looking for Taylor?"

I spin on my heel at the sound of the loud, almost angry voice. I recognize the old lady standing on the sidewalk, leaning on a walker with a Schnauzer on a leash in front of her. It's a small town, after all. There are no strangers. Mrs. Davenport, who lives three doors away, at least she did eight years ago.

"Yes. Do you know where she went, Mrs. Davenport?" I give her a smile. A little charm never hurt. From the way her frown lines only deepen, I guess charm hasn't worked on her since Roosevelt was President. The first one.

"She ran out of here and into the back of a long black car. They practically ran me down." She sniffs like she was hurt when I bet she could kill a bull with that walker of hers.

"You wouldn't happen to know where she was going, would you?"

"Nope," she says and carries on her way. It's not like I need her to tell me, anyway. There's only one other place in town where Taylor would run to. Her hotel is fifteen minutes away, twenty if there's traffic. I grab the muffins—why they matter, I have no idea—and rush back to the car. It's about time for this thing to show me what it's capable of.

I slam my foot on the gas, my hands are clenched around the steering wheel so hard, my knuckles are white. Hell, I don't even have Victoria's number anymore. If I did, I'd call that bitch and ask her what the hell she's been smoking to make her think she had a right to go to Taylor. What the fuck did she tell her? What the hell could she possibly say? Whatever it was, it was enough to make Taylor run away.

When I left, she was laughing and happy and relieved when I told her I wasn't going away for good. A girl didn't turn on a dime like that without any reason. She wouldn't do just the thing she was afraid I would do. If there was an emergency, like something back home, she wouldn't have run away without saying a word. I would've gotten a phone call, a note on the door, something. Not radio silence. Not an empty house.

Victoria always hated Taylor. I can just imagine her going to the house once she knew I wasn't around and telling Taylor all sorts of shit about me, about us being together years ago. I'll never forget those days, when my mother tried everything she could think of to shove Victoria and me into a relationship. It didn't work. I could never get past the fact that she hated Taylor. I couldn't be with someone who bore such malice to the woman I loved.

Besides she wasn't Taylor. As a matter of fact, she wasn't even anybody I liked very much. Even if I couldn't have Taylor, I didn't want some pale copy of her without half the heart or kindness of the original.

I must look like a crazy person when I reach the front desk at the hotel, the car still idling in front of the entrance. The clerk looks at me with mournful eyes. "I'm sorry, Mr. Finley, but she's checked out."

My stomach drops like I'm taking the first drop on a roller coaster. "Excuse me?"

"Yes. You just missed her. She left more than half an hour ago." A shrug, then back to business as usual. He has no idea I'm standing here with my heart somewhere around my ankles.

She has to be at the airport. If she thinks I'm letting her go without a fight, she's out of her mind. I rush back to the car and floor it, tires squealing as I peel out onto the street.

I wasn't kidding when I said I'm not letting her go again.

TAYLOR

W ho is that girl, sitting there in an uncomfortable metal chair in the middle of the airport? I see her in the mirrored wall but I don't know her, and it's not just because she's traveling incognito. Even without the hat and sunglasses, I wouldn't know her. She sits with her shoulders slumped, her spine curved. Her skin is a strange shade of pasty. If I didn't know better, I would think she slathered her face in gray concealer. Why anybody would do that, I don't know, but that's how she looks.

Her mouth too. Both corners hanging down. It pulls the muscles of her cheeks down, too, so she looks a lot older than she is. Are those frown lines? Let's not even discuss the lank hair. Not blow drying will do that.

I shift my body in a feeble attempt to get comfortable. Talk about a waste of time. I'm fairly sure these chairs were designed by torture enthusiasts. I miss the first class lounge, but there weren't any first class seats available on my flight. Maybe I shouldn't have been in such a hurry to take whatever was available first. That would've meant being able to think with a clear head, and I was way beyond that point when I fled my hotel. Now that nearly an hour or so has passed, I'm starting to regret running without getting an explanation.

Like I needed one more thing to regret.

I should have calmly waited at the hotel for him to show up. Then I would have dealt with him in a cold and decisive way. No matter what he said or what explanation his smooth tongue came up with I would know not to forgive him. If he tried to use his hypnotic eyes on me I would just look away. There's not a thing he can do or say to change my mind.

Beside I want to hear the story from his mouth. I want to know why he thought it was all right to use me the way he did. I want to watch him scramble and stutter and try to convince me again that he's a good guy. I want to watch his jaw drop when I tell him I know Victoria is pregnant. It's not fair that he should get off without having to deal with the way he hurt me.

I shake my head and look down at my phone, trying to distract myself. No, being face-to-face with him wouldn't help anything. Having to see him again and remember the way things were last night—the entire time we were together—wouldn't help at all.

I scroll through my Instagram feed and see how many of my so-called friends are living it up right now. One of them is in Bali, another in Hawaii. One of them is currently looking around for a villa on Lake Como. Even the ones who aren't traveling, who take pictures of themselves by the pool or hanging out in their rec room, look like they might as well be staying at a spa. They're all tanned and pampered and fake.

And this is all I have. I close the app before my mood spirals any further out of control.

That's when I hear them. Whispering. They're off to my left, two rows back. Young girls. I can't tell how many there are—they all sound the same. Especially when they're trying to be sneaky. I've been through this more times than I can count, and I learned a long time ago to ignore them until they approach. Ignore them, but be aware of them. It's like having fangirl radar installed in my brain.

Part of me rebels furiously. Is it too much to ask that I be able to suffer in peace? No, I'm not allowed to live my life. It's the public first, me second. I'm falling apart inside, but if those girls were to approach me right now, I would have to put on a smile and pretend that seeing them is the biggest treat in my day. If I didn't, if I frowned or acted tired or distant, I would instantly be classed as arrogant, nasty, bitchy, and too big for my boots. *Taylor doesn't appreciate her fans. Doesn't she realize they made her. Without them she is nothing.*

When I see gossip about other celebrities caught "behaving badly", I always have to wonder what happened to them that day. Why did they act that way? Nobody ever bothers to find out why the celebrity gave a group of screaming fans the cold shoulder. Maybe her dog got sick. Maybe her kid got sick. Maybe she's got a toothache, for Christ's sake.

It's another twenty-five minutes until boarding and I'm antsy as hell. Why can't I just get out of this godforsaken place and get on with forgetting I ever came here? It's like I'm standing in semi-set concrete and I can't lift my feet out of it. It's a special kind of torture.

The whispering gets louder, and there are a few giggles, too. I look straight ahead and wish I hadn't. There's a group of girls outside the gate, looking at me from where they're standing in front of a coffee shop.

I feel like an animal at the zoo. The back of my neck starts getting all hot and prickly. I see one of the girls from the group in front of me look off toward the group behind me and it's like they do some mental telepathy thing because all of a sudden, both groups descend on me like a flock of vultures. It reminds me of that Hitchcock movie, *The Birds*.

There are around ten, maybe twelve of them in all, and all of them are asking me questions at once. My head is spinning and my neck is getting sore from all the swiveling back and forth to smile and exchange a few nice words with them. Their questions overlap, getting louder and louder the longer they try to talk over each other.

They press in on me from all sides: behind, in front, right and left.

TAYLOR

One of them leans over my shoulder and tries to snap a selfie when I'm not ready for one, and I jump when she throws an arm over my shoulder. It's more surprise than anything, but she doesn't take it well. I hear a snide comment, but just barely since all the other chatter is still filling my ears and making my head ache unbearable.

"Guys! Guys! Give me a second, please. I'll take pictures with all of you, just please, let me breathe." I try to stay calm and as positive as possible as I stand up, but they crush in on me. There are dozens more now. Where did they come from?

They're reaching for me, waving at me, trying to touch me. Screaming, crying, shouting, begging for me to get a picture with them. I can't get through. I just want some air. I just want my space back. They start jostling me, begging for something, anything, asking personal questions, getting angry when I don't answer right away but how can I answer when they won't give me a chance to?

One of them grabs at my hat, and my head jerks to the side.

She pulls the hat away and runs off, holding it over her head. I can't go after her, especially since two girls are fighting for my scarf. Problem is, they're pulling it in opposite directions and my neck is caught in the middle.

I can't breathe. Literally this time.

I claw at the fabric and gasp, looking around desperately for somebody to help me. Anybody. This is out of control and I am way outnumbered. I'm going to pass out if they don't stop strangling me.

My dress tears and tears spring to my eyes. One of them ripped my dress. I can't make sense of any of it. They're like a mob. Now I know why Nick always insists on security. I elbow bodies out my way, still choking, though I think one of the girls must have given up because the pressure has eased some. I can draw in a few raspy breaths.

I hear the pounding of footsteps over the screams of my "adoring" fans, and the sight of a half-dozen burly security guards has never been sweeter. Two of them grab me, one by each arm, and rush me off to a private room while the others hold the masses back. I'm so dazed, they almost have to carry me.

"Are you all right, Miss?" They sit me down on a sofa a lot more comfortable than the chairs at the gate. Not that I care anymore about how comfortable the chairs are. All that matters is it's secluded. I unwind my scarf and take deep, shaky breaths while nodding that yes, I'm all right. As all right as I'm gonna be.

I look down at myself. My dress is ripped up the side, almost to the top of my hip. My hair is a straggly, tangled mess. I even lost the elastic holding my braid together. I comb my fingers through and try not to cry. This is what fame has earned me. I can't go to the airport without getting mauled.

"You're Taylor Rose, aren't you?" someone says.

I nod and touch my hands to my throat, which feels raw. Great. I hope they didn't damage my voice. Wouldn't that be ironic? I start shaking.

"Do you want some water?" one of the men asks gently.

I wrap my arms around myself. I just want to go home. I need to be alone for a long time, where nobody can hurt me. I've been mobbed by fans before, but this is on a whole other level. Almost like they hated me. How can you claim to love somebody, then treat them like that?

I'm not human to them. That's how. They look up to me, but I'm not a person. I'm not like them.

"I need to see her! Please!"

My head swivels around at the frantic male voice filtering through the closed door.

"Please, please. I saw what happened. I have to talk to her. Taylor!"

"You're kidding," I croak. I stand and go to the door, still shaky and sore, and press my ear to it.

"I'm a friend of Taylor," Cole babbles. "Please, I know she's in there, I saw you escort her inside after that mob scene. I was just running up. Please, let me see her. I'm worried about her."

"Are you a relative?" a man's voice barks.

"No, but she's my girlfriend. I must see her."

151

"Sorry, Sir, but that's out of the question," the security guard says.

"Taylor! Please! It's Cole!" He really must be desperate if he's screaming at a closed door.

"He can come in," I call out as loud as I can, which isn't very loud at the moment. Then I step back. For a second—the briefest, shortest second—I want to fall into his arms and cry my eyes out. I want him to hold me and protect me and tell me it'll all be okay, that I'm safe. It was all a big mistake and nothing will hurt me so long as he's there. I want all of that. I need it.

But no.

He doesn't deserve to be my hero.

The door opens, and he almost falls into the room. The security guard shoots me a look, and I nod my head with a weak smile. He's only trying to do his job. Cole's eyes are like saucers as he takes in the full sight of me—torn dress, tangled hair, the welt around my throat, my teary eyes.

"Oh, God. Taylor." He reaches for me, just like I knew he would.

I hold up my hands, palms out, and stop him.

His face falls.

"No way. You don't get to touch me. You don't get to do that ever again."

COLE

It's like something out of a nightmare. There I was, running through the terminal, hoping to catch Taylor before her flight left. It was the only flight leaving for LA at that time, so I figured it was a good bet. I heard it before I saw it—the throng of screaming, shrieking girls. It was better than putting a bell on a cat, I thought at the time, and I rushed in the direction of the chaos.

Before I saw the security guards rushing Taylor into a private room across from the gate. When I realized they were hurting her, every protective instinct in my body went into overdrive and my blood ran cold.

Now she doesn't want me to touch her? When she looks like she just got run over by a truck and the only thing that matters is that I get to hold her in my arms and tell her I'll never let her go? She doesn't even want me near her?

"What's all this about, Taylor?" I ask, letting my arms drop to my sides. I need to know why. I let her go once, but never again. "You ran out on me and didn't bother explaining why."

"You think you deserve an explanation?" she rasps. God, she sounds terrible. My eyes roam her face. Her eyes are wide and tormented and there's a welt around her neck. I realize they must have strangled her with her scarf. What the hell is wrong with people? What makes them turn into animals? I wish I could strangle all of them myself. My hands curl into fists, and she notices. "What? Are you going to hit me now?"

I look down and relax my hands. "Listen to yourself. This is me. Have I ever laid a hand on you? I was just angry when I thought about what those girls did to you out there."

"Yeah, well, that's the price I pay, okay? It's the choice I made to lead the life I live and this is the price I pay for success. I can't leave the house without the threat of having my clothes ripped off, or dying by strangulation. No big deal." She wraps her arms around her thin, trembling body and I wonder if she's about to have a breakdown. She sounds like she is.

"Why won't you tell me why you left?"

"You honestly don't know? You mean she didn't tell you?"

"Who is she? Victoria?"

"Oh, so you do know."

I stare at her in amazement. Her eyes are full of hate and she can barely contain her rage. "I looked in through the window of the house and saw her sunglasses on the table. I guessed they were hers, she wears Chanel and there are not too many women who wear designer sunglasses in Black Rock."

"Is this another one of your games, little rich boy?"

I can't believe that she would think a man who worships her

body the way I do could even look at another woman, but I try to put myself in her shoes. She got a real nasty surprise from that evil bitch and she probably thinks I have form for being disloyal or untrustworthy. I remind myself that she doesn't know the real story before I say another word. "I don't know what she said to you, but the last time I saw her was a few months ago at a party where she got drunk and she threw herself at me."

"Oh, is that when she got pregnant?" she asks sarcastically.

My jaw drops. What? This is a surprise I wasn't counting on, but I shouldn't be all that surprised. Victoria was born bitchy. The picture is starting to clear up. I can see exactly what happened. Victoria heard a rumor about me and Taylor. It must have riled her up some because she was obviously waiting outside the house. When I left she took the opportunity to go into the house and confront Taylor with a bunch of lies. Since almost everyone in Black Rock knows the way we broke up eight years ago she knew exactly how to hurt Taylor and make her run. Telling her we're having a baby together. Calling her a homewrecker, and that's just for starters. It all makes sense now. Victoria didn't take into account how tenacious I am. I widen my stance. "She's pregnant? That's news to me."

"Don't lie," Taylor snarls.

"I'm not lying. I have no idea whether or not she's pregnant, but I can tell you with absolute certainty that *if* she is, it *isn't* mine."

"Lying again?"

"It's not a lie. She's the one who is lying! Jesus Christ, Taylor!

Why would you believe that bitch who took every opportunity to make your life miserable over me?"

"Why should I believe you?" she whispers, and there is a thread of hope in her voice.

"Because I love you."

COLE

She shudders. Actually, shudders. "Love? You? You wouldn't know love if it sat up and punched you in the face. So spare me that stinking pile of horse dung. What would Victoria have to gain by coming to me and making up a pile of stories? Why don't you just tell me the truth for once?"

"I am telling the truth! Everything I'm saying is the absolute truth. You know how my parents always wanted for me to get together with her, but I've never been interested. Not in the slightest. I'd rather marry a rattlesnake."

"Yeah, I know," she snarls, grasping on the thing that hurt her the most when we were together. "I was never good enough for your parents."

"I don't care what my parents want, Taylor. This is my life and I want you. Victoria is nothing to me. I don't know why she would do this wretched miserable thing, but I do know she was always jealous of you. Did you not notice how she would copy your hairstyle or how she—"

"Stop, Cole. Just stop." She sits on the couch with her arms still wrapped around herself and rocks back and forth slightly. "I can't deal with this right now. Not all of this at once. I thought it was bad enough when I got here, but now?" She runs a hand through her hair and it trembles. Hard.

"You're right. You shouldn't have to." I want her to be able to rest. I want her to relax and not take all of this on her shoulders at once. She doesn't need, or deserve it. I wish she would let me take care of her.

Instead of calming her down my words only make her hiss with fury. "Shut up. Just shut up, Cole."

It's like a slap in the face.

She looks up at me with a coldness in her eyes that I've never seen before. She's like a different person. "Do you know why it's so easy for me to believe that Victoria was telling the truth about you?"

"No, but tell me." Though in the mood she's in, I almost wish she wouldn't. She could spit fire right now.

"Because I have loved you more than anyone else and you've let me down when I needed you most."

I look at her sadly. "Will you never ever forgive me for that, Taylor?"

"Right. This is not the time to be sarcastic with me."

"I'm sorry, but I don't see how one has to do with the other right now."

"I'll tell you." She stands, and she isn't shaking anymore. "You broke my heart that day, Cole. You left me with nothing."

"Nothing?"

"Nothing that mattered. And what did you do? You couldn't just admit that you were in over your head, and you didn't want what you said you wanted. You had to get drunk to deal with it. Isn't that right? You were so nasty. It was supposed to be the biggest, happiest day of our lives and you destroyed that for me. How can I ever forgive you for that?"

I'm stunned into silence.

She nods and looks at me coldly. "I almost let you get away with it. I did. I was willing to forgive and forget—I mean, it's not like things didn't work out. Now I see that I don't trust you. I would rather take the word of a total bitch over you. If I trust you so little, how can there ever be anything real between us?"

"Taylor, you don't understand."

Her eyes narrow. "I'm about sick to death of you telling me what I don't understand. I understand just fine. Maybe you're the one who doesn't. Did you ever think of that? Do you ever think about how the things you do affect other people? Do you think about anybody but yourself? Did it ever occur to you that you smashed my heart that day?"

"That was a long time ago, Taylor." I know it sounds lame, but it's all I've got right now.

Her face twists and a harsh laugh flies out of her beautiful mouth. "What did you care, anyway? You were set for life. You didn't have to perform for a few shekels. You could sit back, relax, and let Daddy take care of things for you. You had nothing to lose by dropping me flat. You didn't think about that, did you?"

"It's not like that."

"Whatever." She checks the clock on the wall. "I'm boarding soon. You better go."

"Taylor, please." I can't let her go like this. Not like this. Not when we came so close. I take a step forward and she jerks her hand out to warn me not to get any closer.

"Go." Her voice turns my blood to ice.

"I can't leave you like this, with things this way."

She blinks, and her face goes hard. "It doesn't matter. I realized on the way here I don't love you. I don't even like you. I'm glad I left this god forsaken place. For a while I fooled myself, but in the hard cold light of day, there's nothing here for me. You're just wasting your time."

All the air leaves my body in one big gasp, like she sucker punched me. She hadn't said the words, but I thought it was there. I assumed it was. I thought she loved me. I felt she loved me, even if she didn't admit it. There's pain in my chest, radiating all through me. She doesn't love me. It can't be. I couldn't have got it that wrong. She picks up her bag and puts it in her lap, in preparation to go. She's really going to walk out of my life again.

I won't beg. I tried my damndest, but I won't beg. "When you discover the truth in your heart, Taylor, I'll be waiting here for you. Always," I whisper.

She shrugs, looking away, waiting for me to go.

So I do. I walk out of that room and out of her life.

Every footstep takes me one step further away from her. I feel like a man walking his last mile to the electric chair.

That's what it feels like. My life stretches out in front of me, a long gloomy road. What do I have to look forward to in life now that I don't have her?

Before she came back into my life, I fooled myself into believing I was doing all right. That I had it all figured out. I didn't need anybody. I was self-reliant, confident, in charge, in control. I had everything I wanted at the tip of my fingers and life was good. Why did I have to go to her house and turn everything upside down the way I did?

Now, I know the truth. My life is a sham. I can't even pretend it isn't anymore. She's the only thing I want. The happiness, the peace, the connection. She's everything.

She's gone.

I walk back through the terminal and out to my car. The expensive car I used to think was so important. To the life I used to think was so important.

TAYLOR

3 WEEKS LATER

"Thank you, Pittsburgh!" I wave to the audience one last time and let the waves of their adoring energy wash over me. There are moments like this when it's good. It's very good. People spent their hard-earned money to see me perform live, and I gave them the best show I could. As always, I can only hope I gave them their money's worth—the wall of rapturous applause tells me I did.

The moment I'm offstage, one of the stage managers drapes a towel over my shoulders and leads me to my dressing room. There are smatterings of applause all around me as the crew congratulates me and the band on another great show. I thank the band too. Without them I would be singing on an empty stage, probably to no one. I gulp down half a bottle of water before I even reach the dressing room.

There have been nights when I've sweat out three, four pounds during a show, depending on the lighting rig that tour and the amount of movement around the stage. This one is a three-sixty design, so I'm playing to the back as well as to the audience in front of me. I'm always running from here to there, all while trying to sing. My trainer would be proud of how well I did tonight.

One of my strict rules is that I be left alone after a show. I need time to decompress. Sure, there's a lot of adrenaline flowing—especially after a great show—but I can't be around too many people. It's overwhelming after I've already left it all out there onstage. How some people party all night with groupies after giving a three-hour show is beyond me.

The dressing room is a decent size, nicely appointed. I'm used to all sorts of rooms, depending on how nice the arena is. I've crammed myself, my wardrobe and my makeup into rooms the size of a small closet, and I've had entire suites all to myself. This particular room falls right in the middle.

Most singers would have an entourage waiting for them, but I don't like that. Another thing that sets me apart, I guess. I can't see myself keeping a bunch of hangers-on who just want to get what they can from me so that I can appear to have a huge entourage as befits my status as a big time celebrity.

It means I'm alone a lot of the time, but I'm not lonely. I like my solitude. Just last week I wrote the best song I've ever written. I poured all my pain into it and it's good. It's really good.

I open another bottle of water and take my time drinking this one.

"It was a good show. You did great." I stare into my eyes in the mirror and repeat this several times, then smile, but it's an empty smile. It doesn't reach my eyes. They look defeated. Empty. I will always pretend to be happy and upbeat for my fans because I appreciate them. I know they don't have to come out and see me, but they do, so they deserve me at my best. It is hard work pretending and now that I'm alone again, I'm exhausted.

I feel myself deflating like a balloon.

I sigh and sit on the dressing table stool. How much longer am I going to feel this way? It's already been three weeks since the Cole Incident, which is what I'm calling it. Three of the longest weeks of my life. I credit the new tour for pulling me out of it, well to a point, anyway. At least I have an excuse to get out of bed in the morning, and by the time I go to bed I'm too exhausted to do much thinking.

It was much worse before the tour started. I think I spent the first week in bed, pretty much. I would only get out long enough for the maid to change the sheets and freshen things up. Rachael would bring the food that the chef prepared up to me even though I said I didn't want any. She even sat with me one time and waited until I finished an amount she thought was enough.

I know I'm lucky to have such good people in my life. I don't know if they really do but they seem to care. Maybe because I've always tried to be good to them. I didn't know that would come in handy the way it has.

Since that week, I've been doing everything I can to keep myself busy. Always looking for something to distract myself from my issues. I don't know any other way right now. My schedule is all that's keeping me going. I work out to stay in shape so I don't collapse on stage. I eat well so I have the energy for the punishing hours and the energetic dance routines.

That's all I have. My schedule.

I cling to it like a life raft. Sure, I have my friends, but they're hi-bye friends. They're there, but I'm not really sure they have my best interests at heart. I think it's hard to be friends with someone who is more successful. You can't help the envy and jealousy. I don't blame them. If I were in their shoes, I'd probably be jealous of my success too. I forget now, but someone said something very true once. You can have friends or you can have fame and fortune, but you can't have both.

I pull out my cold cream and start taking off the layers of makeup. I always feel more like myself after I take it off. Once that's done, I change out of my show clothes and into sweats, then leave the costume for the costumer to take to the drycleaners.

I sit back down to brush out my hair, but all I want to do is go to sleep. When I'm asleep, I don't have to think about him, or how lonely I am. Or how much I was looking forward to another life with him. He made everything sound so good, so perfect that I started to believe him. I wanted it so much.

Cole Finley created the perfect illusion, but that is all it was. A magic trick by a consummate magician.

I'm right back where I started, and it feels even more empty than it did before. Even with the lights all over and tens of thousands of people chanting my name, my life feels empty. I feel empty.

The knock at the door stirs me out of my miserable trance. "Yes?"

Everybody knows not to bother me unless it's important. It's probably Maria wanting to pick up the costume, but when the door opens, it isn't Maria. It's not my manager, or one of the roadies either reflected in the mirror.

"Catherine?" I can't believe my eyes.

It's been eight years, but she doesn't look a day older than when I last saw her. Just slightly more 'preserved'. She was a beauty in her day and it is from her that Cole inherited his beautiful hazel eyes flecked with gold.

I stand and turn around.

"Hello, Taylor," she says softly, in that deeply cultured voice of hers.

"Come in," I say automatically. I'm just so surprised.

She closes the door and comes into the small room. Her subtle perfume and her expensive shampoo fill the air, scents I've always associated with her.

"What are you doing here?" I'm not unhappy to see her. I didn't care for her husband who was openly hostile, but she kept her feelings about me under wraps. So we always managed to have a cordial relationship.

"I was in town, and I heard you were performing tonight. I couldn't help but come out to see you."

My eyebrows rise. "You saw the show? If I had known you wanted to see it, I would've gotten you box seats, or something."

"That's all right. We have a suite reserved for when we're in town."

"Oh. Of course." I should've known. I always forget how well off they are. I should know better. They don't even live in

Pittsburgh but they have a suite reserved for them here. I guess they do a lot of business here. "Have a seat." I pull up a chair for her. "Would you like something to drink? I could call for some vodka?"

"Oh, no, honey. I didn't come here to put you out like that."

"You wouldn't be putting me out. It's no trouble at all." I go to pick up the phone.

She shakes her head demurely. "That's all right. I don't want to take up much of your time. I know you must be tired after … what's the saying? Leaving it all out there on the stage."

I laugh for the first time in weeks. Ironic how her son broke my heart but she's the one who makes me laugh. "You got it. Very nice."

"Thank you. I still remember some of the lingo from the old days." She sighs, and her beautiful face takes on a bittersweet expression. "It doesn't seem like that long ago, does it?"

"No. It doesn't." Did she come to reminisce? I hope not. I also hope she doesn't want to talk about Cole, but I don't believe for a second that she came to see me perform.

She folds her well-manicured hands in her lap, and they rest on top of her crocodile Birkin bag. She always was stylish. "I feel like the two of us need to talk, Taylor."

TAYLOR

I brace myself. Did the whiny crybaby send his mommy to come talk to me? I wouldn't put it past him.

"I understand you and Cole reconnected after your stepmother's funeral," she says, choosing her words carefully. I can imagine how awkward it must be for a parent to talk about things like this, so I tell myself to give her a break.

"That's right." My voice shakes,

"I'm sorry about your stepmother's passing, by the way. We used to run into each other on occasion. She was always so proud of you."

I have to smile at that. Someone is telling a lie. "That's nice to hear. Thank you."

She nods. "Anyway, as I was saying Cole told me that you two got back together … in a manner of speaking."

"In a manner of speaking," I repeat. "But not really." I feel like we're dancing together. Stepping carefully, back and forth, trying to avoid each other's toes.

"Yes. I understand that, too." She frowns. "I'm sorry things turned out the way they did."

"Yes. Me, too. But that's how things happen sometimes."

"It doesn't have to be that way, you know."

"With all due respect, Catherine, you're not aware of the full situation and it's between Cole and me. I would prefer it stay that way."

"I'm very much aware of the full situation," she argues in the same low, sweet tone of voice. "I think it's you who isn't aware of the true situation and that's why I'm here. There's a lot you don't know, that Cole never told you. He doesn't want to even now. He doesn't know I'm here." She grimaces. "He would be furious with me if he knew."

I can't help it. I'm intrigued. "What is it you want to tell me?"

She takes a deep breath. "Cole told me how upset you still are that he missed your audition eight years ago."

"No, I wouldn't say that. I was upset, but I'm not anymore. Now, I just can't trust him."

"Oh, sweetheart. He never told you, and he made me swear that I wouldn't tell you, either."

I realize I'm holding my breath, waiting to hear what she has to say. "What do you mean? What didn't he tell me?"

"I'm ashamed, even though it wasn't me who did this. It was my husband, but the worst atrocities are not done by just the evil perpetrators, but the good people who stand by and do nothing. I stood by and did nothing. I know now, I shouldn't have. I destroyed my son's life. I hope you can forgive me." She looks at the floor. It's the only time in all the years I've known her that I've seen her too ashamed to look somebody in the eye. "My husband told Cole that if he skipped the audition and went to work for him, he would make sure you became a star."

I scowl. That doesn't make sense. "Your husband would never go out of his way like that for me."

She closes her eyes and shakes her head at my naivety. "He didn't do that for you, Taylor. It was to keep Cole away from you." She winces. "I'm so sorry. It sounds terrible."

It all dawns on me. I'm surprised a lightbulb doesn't go off over my head. My heart is beating so fast I hear my blood rushing in my ears. "So he forced Cole to skip the audition?"

"That's right. He didn't say it in so many words, he didn't need to. My husband lives in Black Rock, but don't make the mistake of underestimating him. He is an extremely powerful figure with vast influence in the financial, political, and entertainment worlds. His tentacles spread from Washington to Hollywood. He only had to insinuate that he could have kept you from achieving your dreams, and Cole would have understood exactly what that meant."

"Oh. I see," I enunciate slowly, even though I don't see anything! I can't understand how his father can hate me so much. I have never done anything bad to him.

"That was why Cole was in such a shameful state when you saw him that morning. He must've been utterly devastated. He had to get roaring drunk just so he could bring himself to let you down."

"I don't understand why he made an agreement like that. He didn't have to. We could've made it together. I'm sure we could have. Unless ... unless his father would've sabotaged him, as well."

There is no hesitation in her. "He would have. Not out of spite, but because he wants something else for Cole. He didn't care what Cole wanted only what he did. Cole is his only son so he needs Cole to take over his empire. My husband thinks he can control everything and everyone. Well, maybe he can."

I can't get it all together. Cole, drunk the afternoon of the audition. Telling me he didn't want to be part of my life anymore. So nasty. His words still sting, all these years later. It was all because ... "Because he wanted me to have my dream," I whisper, trembling.

"Yes. Don't you see? He wanted you to be happy. It meant more to him than even his own happiness. He had to let go of his greatest dream. You. Because he wanted you to have yours. He was willing to do anything for you."

"He wanted to be famous, too?"

"Maybe, but not as much as he wanted you, Taylor. He was so in love with you, but his father wouldn't allow it. This was his way of splitting you two up. For good."

I nod slowly, thinking it all over, the shock subsiding, and unbelievable euphoria bubbling into my heart. "And he just about succeeded."

TAYLOR

The whole world shifts on its axis. I don't know what to think about anything. Eight years of seeing things one way, and now this.

"This all seems unreal." I pace the floor and rub my clammy palms on my pants. "I mean, isn't this all a little convenient? After eight years, and after telling Cole off for ditching me that day, it suddenly comes out that he was acting in my best interest?"

"Yes, I realize it seems convenient, but that doesn't make it any less true. I told Cole to be honest with you even at the time, but he refused, not just because it would hurt you, but he was afraid you would skip the audition too and give up your dream. He didn't want you to play small-time gigs for the rest of your life."

I can't argue with that. I would've skipped the audition and told that bastard to go straight to hell. "I always knew he didn't think I was good enough for Cole, but I didn't think he would go that far. So your husband somehow, what?

Convinced the record company to sign me? Was sort of my agent behind-the-scenes? Did he grease palms or something?" I feel dirty. There I was, thinking I made it based on my talent. And now I find out it was all set up for me. I feel a cross between disgust and dismay.

"Your talent got you as far as you've come, Taylor. You don't ever have to question that. But let me ask you this: how do you think a girl as beautiful as you managed to reach the top as quickly as you did without a single moment spent on the casting couch? Hmmm?"

I gasp. Something niggles at the back of my mind, things I've overheard, secret whispers about dark parties full of insiders that I've never been invited to, but I still don't want to believe her. I can't believe her. "The casting couch is for Hollywood not for the music business," I say scornfully.

A strange expression crosses her face. "Fame and fortune always comes at a great price, Taylor. There are millions of young girls with great talent and yet only a few are picked out to be superstars, what do you think informs the selection process?"

Now that I look back, everything was so easy, if I am honest even too easy. Doors opened that I didn't even knock on, because I didn't know they existed. It all fell into place like it was meant to be, or like it was arranged for me.

"Why didn't Cole tell me all this three weeks ago? Why let me walk away thinking he was at fault?"

"Because he didn't want to take anything away from you. He didn't want you to think less of your achievement."

I stare at her in horror. "My god, he must really, truly love me."

"Yes, he does. His love is much purer than I ever imagined."

"Will his father accept me now?"

"No. You will never be acceptable to my husband. He wanted Cole to date and hopefully marry somebody, how do I say this? From our kind." She winces. I can only imagine how uncomfortable it is for her, talking about her husband like this. She's nothing if not loyal. To a fault, sometimes.

"Let me guess, someone like Victoria."

She nods, wrinkling her nose. "Yes."

My mood darkens. "Did they ever?"

"Never. At first I thought she would make a good candidate, but Cole couldn't stand her."

"So, they were never engaged?"

"Most certainly not."

"And she's not pregnant with his baby?"

"Unless she found one of his used condoms somewhere and used a turkey baster."

At any other time I would have laughed, but not now. "You don't know how relieved you've made me. I mean that. Thank you for this." I cross my hands over my chest and just about burst out sobbing. "I wish Cole had told me a long time ago. I feel so bad. I accused him of being disloyal and unreliable and he has actually been as unshakeable as a rock the whole time."

She only shakes her head. "Oh, no, sweetheart. Don't feel bad. What is past is past, but both of you are still so young. You have your whole lives in front of you."

"Do you think Cole will forgive me? I was very horrible to him at the airport. I think I really hurt him."

"There is nothing you can do to stop Cole from loving you. He sacrificed his own happiness so you could achieve your dreams. Even though he is a wreck now, he didn't want me to tell you the truth. He did not ever want you to question your talent or wonder whether you deserve the fame you have found. He wanted you to believe you did it all on your own."

I stare at her speechlessly. Cole didn't break his promise. All those years I thought he did.

Catherine shrugs. "I am afraid I just undid all his work, but I felt it was important to both of you. What you do after this is up to you, but I have done my part. I hope you can forgive me."

"Forgive you?" I go to her and throw my arms around her neck. "I can't thank you enough!" Questioning where my fame comes from means nothing, nothing to me compared to being without Cole, thinking he didn't care about me, thinking he lied.

She hugs me back, then smiles up at me. "I'm flying back tonight on our jet. Do you want to come with me?"

Do I? "Yes. More than anything."

TAYLOR

It's nearly two in the morning by the time Catherine's driver pulls up in front of Cole's house. I can't believe the way my heart is racing. I'm nervous and I'm excited and I'm happy and I'm scared all in one.

"You're sure he'll forgive me?" I whisper, wringing my hands.

"There's nothing to forgive. It's not your fault. Both of you were just pawns on my husband's chessboard."

"You're right. I just hope he sees it that way."

"Something tells me he will."

"How do you know?"

"I'm his mother. I know these things. Now get out there and knock on the door." She gives me a playful shove and I get out of the car. My heart is throbbing harder than ever. What if he doesn't want to see me? What if?

He doesn't give me time to worry.

As soon as I ring the bell, he throws open the door, our eyes connect, and he practically pulls me off my feet and into the house. Before I know it, I'm in his arms and he's kissing me like there's no tomorrow. I'm kissing him back with tears streaming down my face.

"I'm sorry. I'm so sorry." It's all I can get out between kisses, and I'm so breathless, I can barely even whisper the words. He doesn't seem to care. He's kissing my face, my mouth, my forehead, my chin.

"I've missed you so much." His arms are like steel bands around me, but I don't mind. I never want him to let go again.

"I've missed you," I sob. "You have no idea how much. I'm so sorry, I was so harsh. I made such a mistake. I made such a mistake."

"No, no. You did the best you could. It's all right. I'm so proud of you." He pulls back to look at me, and there's a brilliant smile on his face. "I love you, Taylor Rose McCarthy."

It's like the clouds have opened and the sun is shining through. "I love you! I do love you. I was lying when I said I didn't. I'm sorry. I'm so sorry."

"Stop saying sorry. You don't have to apologize anymore. I mean it. It's all right. You haven't done anything wrong." He holds my face in his hands. "It's all right."

"Can I ask you a favor?"

"Of course." he smiles, stroking my cheeks with his thumbs.

"Can we close the door and sit down?" We've been standing

in the open doorway all this time. His laughter rings in my ears.

"Yeah, come on in, even though I actually want everybody seeing you out here and getting the wrong idea…"

COLE

I t's like a dream coming true. One minute, I was sitting here, trying to lull myself to sleep by watching a brainless movie. The next, she came to the door.

And that was it.

Everything changed.

Everything.

I can't stop touching her. It's like I still can't quite believe she's real. She's never going back. If I touch her, she's really here. Finally. She must feel the same way, since she's doing the same thing.

"I guess you must've talked to my mother," I say.

"Hey! If I hadn't, would I be here? She was only being a mom. It took guts to come to me the way she did—she was sure you would kill her."

"I'm not sure I won't," I growl.

"Aren't you glad I'm here?" she smiles.

"Of course. It's my stupid ego getting in the way." I roll my eyes with a shrug. "I'm just a stupid man. What can I say?"

"Yeah, well, I've been a foolish woman." She shakes her head with a frown. "I should've known you wouldn't hurt me the way I thought you did."

"You're not a mind reader," I remind her. "You couldn't have known."

"You were stubborn."

"I thought I was doing the right thing. I'll stand by that til the day I die."

She squeezes my hand. "I know. I'm not sure if I should thank you or slap you."

"As long as you slap me the right way," I suggest, raising an eyebrow, and she giggles. I've missed that giggle. It's like balm for my soul.

"I mean it, though. I know you did it for the right reasons, and I love you for it, but you knew that was what stood between us—that day, the audition. Why didn't you tell me at the airport?"

"I wanted to," I admit, "but would you have believed me? Be honest. Would you have accused me of making up stories?"

She grimaced. "Yeah. I guess I would have. I wasn't in my right mind that day."

"Who would be? You were attacked." I wrap my arms around her the way I wanted to that day and she rests her head on my shoulder. "I'm so sorry about that."

"It's an occupational hazard," she murmurs, snuggling up

against me. She smells like a funny mixture of hairspray, makeup, and sweat.

"Did you have a show tonight?" I ask.

"Yeah. Were you following along with me?"

"No. I can just tell you were performing."

She straightens up, gasping. "Oh, my God! I probably stink!"

"You don't stink," I laugh, "but you don't smell the way I'm used to smelling you, is all. God, you must be exhausted. Performing, flying here …"

"It's no worse than moving on to a new city right after a show," she points out.

That gets me thinking. "You're not missing a new stop on the tour for me, are you?"

She shakes her head. "I have two days off, then it's on to Philadelphia. As far as I'm concerned, I'll never go back out there again."

"Philadelphia?"

"Tour." Her voice is firm, and her face is stony.

"Are you sure you mean that? Didn't you just get started?"

"I'm not as happy doing anything as I am when I sit here with you right now. We have each other, finally. Why would I want to go back on tour and ruin that?"

"You could never ruin that, no matter how hard you tried." I cup her chin in my palm. "You don't have to worry about me. You only have to worry about whether or not you're really happy."

"You know I'm not." She sighs. "But I did make a commitment, and I have twenty cities left to go."

"Wow. Twenty. I don't know how you do it."

She grins. "I could do it standing on my head. I'm not concerned with the length or the number of cities."

"What are you concerned with?"

"Not having you. You're what I've been missing all this time. I was too shy to tell you that before, when we were together. It's all you." She shrugs as tears fill her eyes. "When we performed together at Artie's, it was like all the old feelings came back. I remembered why I used to love doing this. I got back what I was missing all along."

"So what are you saying? I should get up there on stage with you?"

"No. You know that's not what I mean."

"Oh, so you're trying to hog the spotlight?"

"Shut up!" She gives me a playful shove, then gets serious again. "I don't know what I'm saying. I just want to be with you, is all. Knowing you're in my life and that at the end of the tour, I'll be coming back to you, will go a long way."

"What if I meet you whenever I can, wherever you happen to be? I can't guarantee that I can follow you around everywhere, but …"

"You mean, you can't be my groupie?" she smirks.

"I've always wanted to be a groupie, too. Damn. But I'll do the best I can."

Her smile is radiant. "That would be amazing."

"Then, it'll happen. Whatever you need. After this tour—well, we'll talk about what happens next. I'll stand by whatever you want to do."

"Thank you." She winds her arms around my neck and squeezes tight, then chuckles. "I guess I'd better take a shower if I want to keep climbing all over you like this."

"Mm, climbing all over me. That sounds good. Maybe I'll join you?"

She stands and takes me by the hand, then giggles. "Here I am, trying to be seductive, but I don't know where the bathroom is."

"I'll lead the way," I chuckle, and we go upstairs together. While I'm turning on the shower, she takes off her clothes. Hallelujah. I didn't think I would ever get to see or touch her again, but here she is. In my bathroom, about to get into the shower with me. If I'm dreaming, I don't want to wake up.

Minutes later, we're soaping each other up and making a huge mess, laughing through it all. Our laughter fades as we start touching more interesting places, and before I know it we're wrapped in each other's arms, leaning against the shower wall. I don't know what's hotter—her or the water.

"I love you," she whispers into my mouth before covering it with hers, kissing me until it hurts. I give it right back to her, while one of my hands slides over her slick skin until it finds its place between her legs.

"I love you, too," I groan, then set about the job of making her come like she never has before. It's a tough job, but somebody's got to do it.

From now on, it'll only be me.

COLE

One week later

"I'm home," I call as I come in through the front door. "Are you there?"

The house is silent, and my brow furrows. Usually she comes to the door to greet me. A feeling of unease settles in my stomach.

"Taylor?"

"Can you come up, please?" she calls, her voice coming from the bedroom upstairs. Relief floods through my body. I have to learn to relax. We're together now. Nothing will go wrong. I follow her voice and run up the stairs. What is going on here? At the doorway, I stop.

I see exactly what's going on.

She is laid out on the bed, completely naked, her legs are

spread, and her hand between her legs as she plays with her pussy. My jaw drops. She looks incredible and she knows it. She smiles at me and slides to the end of the bed, standing up, and twirling around as she approaches me.

"What's this in aid of?" I ask, and she shrugs.

"Can't I treat my man after a long day?" she murmurs, and plants a gentle kiss against my lips.

I am already hard, already dizzy with how badly I want her. She pulls back and I catch her hand, the one that's been between her legs, and pull it to my mouth. I suck on her fingers, one at a time, tasting her, savoring the sweetness of her scent on my tongue. She bites her lip and watches me.

"Don't move," she orders, and slides to her knees in front of me.

I watch as she undoes my belt, and makes quick work of pulling down my pants and my underwear. She doesn't take her eyes away from mine once. The lust in her gaze has my cock rock hard and throbbing. She slowly wraps her hand around my erection and turns her attention to it, flicking her tongue out against her lips as though she can barely restrain herself.

Then she raises her gaze to look at me, as though asking for permission, and her sweet submissiveness mixed with her seductive sexuality is almost enough to get me to blow my load right there and then. With a secret smile, she leans forward and sucks me into her mouth.

"Fuck," I growl, cupping her head with my hand and holding her in place.

Not that she is going anywhere. No.

She slides her mouth down my entire length in one smooth motion, her mouth sweet and hot. It feels amazing, as she works her tongue up the underside of my cock, along the sensitive seam that sends a shiver pulsating up my entire body. I notice her hand has found its way between her legs again, and feel my cock grow even harder between her lips at the thought this is getting her off so much she had to find some relief.

"I wish I could watch you," I murmur, and she pulls her mouth off me with a soft "pop"; a thin line of saliva keeps us attached, a reminder of where she'd just been. She looks up at me with a deviant smile.

"I have an idea," she murmurs, and I raise my eyebrows.

"Oh yeah?"

She climbs back on to the bed, flipping on to her back, and shifts so that her head is right at the edge of the bed. She motions for me to come closer, tilting her head back, and draws me into her mouth at that angle, at the same time sliding her hand back down between her legs to stroke her clit.

"Holy shit," I breathe, my eyes tracing her naked body as my cock slips back into her mouth, and down her throat. At this angle, she can take me even deeper, allowing me to thrust gently into her. Her hips writhe back and forth on the bed as she grinds against her hand, and the sight of her losing herself to this the same way I am is beyond hot. I etch the scene into my memory, along with the incredible sensations. She slides a hand around my thigh and draws me in closer, shifting her head, and before I know it she is deep-throating me, my cock buried deep inside her mouth as she hungrily works her tongue against me.

Even after all this time I cannot believe my luck. A year ago who would have thought that I would be coming home to be deep-throated by this beyond-sexy woman as she fingers her swollen clit for my viewing pleasure? It doesn't get much better than this.

She begins to move her hand with more purpose, and I thrust a little harder; I'm getting close. She pushes me a way a little, so she can speak, and I let her.

"Come on my tits," she breathes, a demand I'd never expect to hear from her but that I'm all too happy to oblige; her breasts are amazing, small and pert and always tempting, and she leans her head down to take my balls into her mouth while I stroke myself over her. She is rocking her hips rhythmically now, hitting her stride, and she is letting out these soft little moans against my skin as she traces her tongue around my balls. The sights, the sounds, the sensations – it is all too much. I stroke my cock once more and it explodes, coating her breasts as she finds her own release below me.

My cock pulses a few times before I relax once more, a slight ringing in my ears like I am returning from another dimension. She slides herself back up the bed and I slide forward to join her.

"Holy shit," I murmur, closing my eyes and letting my head fall against the pillow. "That was amazing."

"Glad I can treat you." She giggles, and I turn to her, this crazy-sexy deviant who has just made me come not ten minutes after I walk through the door.

"Maybe I can return the favor?" I suggest, tracing a finger across her hipbone. She shivers.

"Let's take a shower first," she suggests, getting to her feet. "And then we'll see ... if I want to sit on your face."

I get up and follow her at once. I don't need telling twice. I land a playful slap on her ass, and she shoots a grin over her shoulder at me.

EPILOGUE

TAYLOR

Two Years Later

The rain patters against the window, providing the perfect background music as I curl up in my chair, my feet up on an ottoman. There's a warm, soft blanket over my legs and a cup of tea beside me. In my hands is a big, thick book from my library.

I'm in heaven, in other words.

I glance out the window, at the dark storm clouds coming in. I couldn't be happier about it. There's no place I'd rather be than in my chair by the window, in the little space I claimed as my sitting room when we bought this house around a year ago.

It's been a wild, beautiful ride since then. I've never owned a house before, not one like this, anyway. Not a house where I didn't have a cook and a maid and a series of landscapers and a bunch of other luxuries. We do have help, a housekeeper comes in twice a week, but that's a far cry from having twenty-four/seven service. We do have landscapers come out to do the big jobs, like cutting back tree branches, since the house is surrounded by big, beautiful trees. An experienced old gardener came around a few weeks once to help me with the more arduous jobs. But I'm the one who does the weeding and watering and seeding. I'm the one who gets my hands dirty. I love every minute of it.

I love every minute of my life.

I lean my head back against the soft, plush chair and smile when I think about what a culture shock those first few months were for me. I wasn't used to loading the dishwasher, doing the laundry, cooking the meals, or doing the grocery shopping. Yes, I did all those things when I was a teenager, but it's funny how quickly a girl can fall out of the habit when she's used to having everything done for her. There I was, for all those years, thinking I was down-to-earth and normal.

Cole didn't want me playing housewife, but I insisted on doing as much on my own as I could. No more personal assistants for me. I have to say he tried hard to make me change my mind, but I stuck to my guns. I was determined, and in the end I got the hang of domestic life. Cole stuck around through it all, which makes him the most patient man in the world. He even managed to choke down my first few attempts at cooking dinner.

"I'm sorry!" I said the first night, as I chucked most of a meal down the garbage disposal. "The most I ever cooked was a boxed mac and cheese."

"That would be an improvement right now," he made the mistake of commenting.

I know he was trying to make light of the situation, but that turned out to be a very … well … let's just call it, interesting night. It took me a very short time to make him admit that he was no great shakes at cooking, either. The next morning, I went out to get a couple of cookbooks and walked myself through the finer points of cooking. Now, it's one of my favorite things to do. It relaxes me the way gardening and reading does.

Which reminds me that I have to get dinner started. It's a special night. I hate to leave the comfort of my reading nook, but Cole's favorite dinner is my spinach and goat cheese stuffed chicken breasts with pasta alfredo and artichoke heart salad. Yes, I've come a long way in a short time.

I walk down the stairs and pass through the airy, spacious living room with its fireplace and pocket doors, original to the house. God, I love this house. A big, rambling farmhouse built in the late 1800s, still with so much of its original charm. The kitchen ceiling is overlaid in pressed tin and the hardwood floors are original. In almost every room there are fireplaces with intricately carved mantles I could stare at for hours. I did too, when we first moved in.

I turn on the sound system in the den, which is only separated from the kitchen by an island. What I love most about this place are the renovations the previous owners put in. They're all respectful of the house's original architecture, but serve to completely open it up. I turn on my favorite piece of music and start cooking, singing along as I do. Maybe I should incorporate a few jazzy tunes into my next show …

I'm hard at work, rolling pounded chicken breasts around the garlicky goat cheese filling when I hear the front door open. "Oh, shoot! I didn't know you were getting home early tonight, or I would've started this sooner."

"Oh, it's okay." I hear Cole's footsteps as he walks down the hall and into the kitchen, which sits at the opposite end of the house. "Wow, you're really cooking tonight! I didn't expect all this!"

"Well, it's a special night, you know."

"It is?" I'm glad I have my back to him so he can't see the way I roll my eyes.

"Yes!" I plop the last breast into the baking pan and turn to wash my hands. "I thought we could use a special dinner."

"Would these look good on the table?" He steps up behind me and slides an arm around me, revealing a bouquet of blood-red roses.

"You remembered!" I'm laughing as I turn around to give him a hug. I should've known he wouldn't forget.

"Of course. It's been two years since that night at my old house. One of the best nights of my life."

"Me, too." I hold his face in my hands as I kiss him, then giggle when I leave wet handprints there. "Sorry," I murmur as I wipe his cheeks with my apron. I take the flowers and pull a vase from the cupboard.

"Hey, I was talking with Artie today." He sits on one of the stools on the opposite side of the island, facing me. "He wanted to know if you're free in two weeks for a gig."

"Two weeks? Yeesh. I don't know. Did you look at the schedule?"

"Yeah. You have two more that week, and three the next."

"You know that's my cut-off." I shoot him a look.

"I know, I know. I told him you'd get back to him."

"Why does he call you and not me?" I ask, popping a piece of artichoke heart into my mouth.

"Because he knows I'm a soft touch … and you're a soft touch for me." He opens his mouth, and I expertly toss a piece of artichoke in there.

"Yeah, yeah. He's right. I'll do it on one condition."

"What's that?" The way he arches one eyebrow tells me he knows just what I'm about to say.

"I want you up there with me."

"No."

"Then, no. See? Wasn't that easy?" I slide the chicken into the oven and go back to making the sauce for the pasta.

"Oh, that's not fair," he whines.

"That's life, baby. Show business. Take it or leave it." I leave it. For the most part, anyway. I still perform up to three times a week in small bars and clubs around the area, but I sing my songs, my way. My manager thought I was insane, obviously, the way he thought I was insane when I sold the house and let the staff go and told my band it was the end of the road. My guitarist and keyboard player appear with me from time to time, when they're in the area, but the rest went on to other jobs. They're all good enough to play with just about anybody.

By the time the food's ready, Cole has the table set and I place the crystal vase of roses in the center. "They're just gorgeous. Thank you, sweetie."

"Of course." He slides his arms around my waist and pulls me in for a deep, lingering kiss that just about curls my toes. I let myself melt into him for a moment, winding my arms around his neck, pressing my body to his. It's almost enough to make me forget about dinner.

Then, I remember why this dinner is so special. "I'd better bring the food out before we sweep everything off the table and use it for something else," I murmur, which makes him laugh. He helps me bring the food over and pulls out my chair with a flourish. I flutter my eyelashes and sit down, while he picks up a bottle of white wine and holds it over my glass.

"No wine for me, thanks." I hold my hand over the top of the glass. He shrugs and pours it for himself.

"No wine? With pasta? Since when?" He sits down across from me and pulls in his chair, then spreads a napkin across his lap. It isn't until he picks up his knife and fork that my meaning dawns on him. Meanwhile, I'm sitting here, waiting for him to get the hint. He's adorably dense sometimes.

His jaw drops. "I don't want to go jumping to conclusions, but are you …"

I nod, biting my lip. I hope he wants this baby. I've been aching to tell him about it all day. "I'm pregnant. I went to the doctor this morning to confirm."

There go the knife and fork, clattering to the floor. For a second, I'm pretty sure he's going to join them. "Are you okay?" I whisper, suddenly terrified.

Slowly, so slowly, a smile spreads across his face. It's like watching the sun rise in speeded up video, all of a sudden, everything's bright. "Okay? Are you kidding?" He's out of his chair in the blink of an eye and kneeling beside me. "Everything's all right with you, right?"

"Yes. Everything's fine. I'm in great shape."

He takes my hands. "A baby. Our baby."

"You're happy?"

"Do I look happy?" He laughs and a tear spills down his cheek. I reach up to wipe it away.

"I'm so glad. I'm happy, too, by the way."

We're both laughing and crying and I've never been so over-joyed, ever. It's like the last piece of my life is falling into place. A family.

"Catherine called earlier. I felt bad not telling her, I didn't want her to know before you."

"We call her together after dinner, okay?"

I smile. "Yes. I owe so much to her."

He looks down at my still-flat stomach. "Hey, in there. I love you, little baby."

"He or she is about the size of a blueberry right now," I tell him, stroking his hair.

He grins up at me. "Blueberry. That's a nice name."

"Don't you dare."

"What? Don't all celebrity musicians name their kids all kinds of off-the-wall names?"

"Yeah, well, I'm not a celebrity anymore. I'm just me." *Mommy*, I whisper to myself. I'd rather be Mommy than the world-famous Taylor any day of the week.

"Is there anything I can do for you?" he asks, jumping to his feet as he suddenly becomes Mr. Concerned Dad.

"You can do one thing," I suggest.

"What?"

I wink. "You can let me eat this dinner. I'm eating for two now, you know."

The End

Too Hot
to Handle

RIVER LAURENT

Too Hot To Handle

978-1-911608-18-9

ACKNOWLEDGMENTS

Thank You,
Brittany Urbaniak

MADISON

"Oh, come on, you know it's going to be fun!"

"I'm just not sure," I rolled my eyes at my best friend, Eleanor, who was sitting opposite me with a look on her face that told me she was never going to take no for an answer.

"It's precisely what you need right now." She nudged my foot with hers beneath the table. "A bit of fun, yeah?"

"I think it's more fun for you than for me," I said, taking a sip of my coffee and shaking my head.

She leaned back and observed me for a moment, before letting out a long sigh, obviously trying to figure out how she could best twist my arm. "Well, since I'm right off of a break-up." she nodded pointedly. "I get one wild night on the town with you, no questions asked, right?"

"I guess so." I finished my coffee and fiddled with the sugar packets on the table in front of me, arranging them in parallel lines. "It just doesn't sound like my kind of thing, though."

"What? Hot guys aren't your kind of thing?" She was the one rolling her eyes now. She reached into her bag and pulled out a slightly crumpled brochure, and laid it out on the table in front of me, smoothing out the creases.

"What are you, their PR person now?" I teased.

She waved her hand enthusiastically at me. "Just look at this guy," she said as she stabbed her finger onto the paper. "Chad Weston. How can any woman with blood running in their veins not want to see him in person?"

"That leaves me out. I have coffee running mine."

She sighed elaborately as if I was too much for her to put up. I looked down at the man she was pointing to. Okay, I had to admit, he was swoon-worthy hot. Well, they were hardly going to put some plain guy on the front of the brochure advertising their male strip show, were they? Even so, his bright green eyes and mess of brown hair were cute, and that big-ass grin was almost as distractingly attractive as his ripped abs and muscular arms.

"I guess he's pretty hot," I shrugged.

She threw her hands dramatically in the air, attracting the attention of a few people sitting around us. That wasn't a problem for her. She liked attention, loved it when she was the center of attraction. *"Pretty hot?"* she squealed. "Do you know they call him Subway Chad."

I frowned. "Subway Chad?"

"Don't play coy. Haven't I seen you eating their twelve inch sandwiches before."

I flushed bright red. "Oh, that."

She smirked. "Yes, that. Don't you agree it will be worth seeing? You've never seen one that big have you."

I swallowed hard. Now I was certain everyone was looking at me as if I was some kind of freak. "No," I croaked.

"So, you're going to come with me?"

"I don't know, El. It's really not my thing."

"Come on. What would you do otherwise. Bury your face in one of those ridiculous books of yours?"

I bit my lip. That was exactly what I planned on doing. "What's your game-plan? Just look at them until you get over Jonathan?"

"Nope," She grinned widely. "I'm going to get that American dude into my bed. It's my life work."

"What, ever since you saw this brochure, you mean?"

The sarcasm was lost on her. She nodded. "Ever since."

"So you down for it?"

I gave a long sigh. I guess it wouldn't kill me to go out with her for one night. "What time does it start?"

"Seven, and I promise you won't be disappointed," she said nodding at me pointedly. "You never know you might get to go home with one of the other men in the troupe."

"I don't think so," I fired back immediately.

"Why not? It'll just be a one night stand. You know, just let yourself go with a perfectly gorgeous God of a man."

I was not the kind of girl men who looked like that would chose to take home for the night. I carried a bit too much weight around my hips and thighs and I had the kind of face you would miss in a crowd. I was a plain Jane. In all probability I would be taking a taxi home on my own, which actually suited me just fine. "I'll come by your place and meet you at half-six."

"Not necessary. I have got the transport all sorted out. I'll come pick you up at half-six." She got to her feet, and leaned in to drop a quick kiss on the side of my cheek. "Come on, we need to go and get you a dress."

"I have plenty of dresses," I protested. "I don't need any more."

"Trust me, what you have at home isn't going to do it for an event like this," She pulled me to my feet. "We're going shopping."

MADISON

"Fine," I got to my feet reluctantly. Hanging out with Eleanor these days left me feeling more exhausted than ever; she was always running around, dragging me to this and that even, as though just my company alone wasn't enough for her anymore. Now that she had split with Johnathan who she had been with for almost a year, I had to come to terms with the fact that I was going to be seeing a lot more of her than I had been before. In the past she tended to get obsessed with dudes, getting stuck on them at the expense of nearly everything else in her life and needing me to offload on, but at least with this stripper, Chad What's-his-name, he would be out of the city by the end of the night.

Although, I had to admit, I was a little cynical about her chances of hooking up with him, anyway. How many women must throw themselves at him all the time? I mean, Eleanor was beautiful, with slim hips, a wasp waist, and bee-stung lips that seemed to have men falling at her feet, but this guy got women hot for a living. It wasn't like he could be short on them.

"Oh, I'm so looking forward to this." She was practically prancing down the street as she peered into the windows of shops we passed by, to find something that looked good on me. I really didn't want to get anything new, but if it would make her happy and help get her mind off the break-up, then I wasn't sure I, as a best friend, was allowed to argue. Even though it often felt as though we'd gone in different directions these last few years, I still felt this sense of duty towards her.

"Ooh, what about that one?" She pointed at a blue dress in the window of a shop I knew just by looking would be way out of my price range. The dress looked pretty good on the mannequin, but I wasn't sure how it would go on me – the deep blue was a pretty color, and I liked the sweetheart neckline that looked smart and not too over-the-top. Like something I could wear to work.

"I guess we could give it a go," I replied gamely, and we headed in to try it on.

The shop was part of a big shopping center. There was a bookshop sitting next to it that I glanced longingly over at. God, if I could just duck in there for five minutes... I never regretted blowing a big portion of my paycheck on books, even if my sister always mocked me for it. Not that I had much of a paycheck these days, the company I'd done sales for two years just shut down last month. That's part of the reason I didn't want to drop all this money on a dress, or on tickets for this show tonight. I didn't have it to spare. But I would do what I had to, to help Eleanor.

"Come on, try it on!" she urged as soon as she'd found a version of the dress in my size.

I took it from her and slipped into it in the changing rooms, trying not to look at myself too closely in the mirror. It wasn't that I hated my body or anything. No, I just didn't find much use for it these days. I hadn't dated anyone in a long time, and, not being one for one-night-stands, that pretty much meant that I hadn't had sex for a very long time. Also, I had put on some weight. I knew that my hips were wider and my thighs softer than they had been before. It bothered me enough to want to try and pretend it wasn't happening.

I looked up once the dress was zipped around me, and I twisted back and forth in front of the mirror while I tried to figure out whether I liked it or not. It certainly wasn't *bad*. The blue popped against my dark hair, and it cinched in a few bits of me that needed it, but it wasn't precisely *good* either. It just sort of *was*.

"You dressed in there?" Eleanor called, and before I could reply she had whipped the curtain back. She looked me up and down and nodded slowly, as though this was exactly what she'd had in mind.

"Yeah, that's perfect," she grinned up at me. "Don't you think?"

"Uh, it's okay," I nodded. "Not...not really much, to be honest."

"Once you're all done up for going out you'll feel different," she promised with some authority. "You should definitely buy it."

"You think?" I asked doubtfully.

"For sure," she replied firmly.

I glanced down at the tag hanging off the hip and winced once more. The tickets for this place were going to be expensive too, I knew that, and then there would be the taxi there and back and the overpriced drinks at the venue…

"Stop worrying," Eleanor clicked her fingers in my face, pulling me back to the real world. "It's all going to be fine, alright?"

"Alright," I conceded.

Shooing her out of the dressing room I took another look at myself in the mirror. Yeah, I guess the dress looked okay. I had seen myself look better, but that was before I put on all that weight. Also, I just wasn't used to seeing myself dressed up. It had been more than a month since I'd had to go into the office with anything resembling a nice outfit on. Most of these days, I sat around in my apartment in jeans and a baggy sweatshirt, reading and cooking and jumping every time the phone rang in case it was someone wanting to offer me a job interview. It never was.

The job market was as rewarding, it seemed, as the dating one.

I bought the dress and watched as the saleslady careful folded it in tissue before slipping it into a bag. Fortunately, the one pair of heels that I owned were black and would go with it.

Eleanor was practically skipping along beside me, she was so excited about the rest of this evening. It was starting to get dark, the light leaking from the sky, just like the hope that I had any chance of getting out of this event which was about as far removed from 'me' as it could possibly be.

"I wonder what he'll be like in bed," she wondered, like it was just a matter of time before she found out.

I bit my tongue to keep from pointing out to her that this hook-up wasn't a given quite yet. If she wanted to have her little fantasy no good would come for me to shit all over that. I just smiled and nodded along. Might as well get used to it. I was going to have to listen to that for the rest of the night.

MADISON

An hour later I was back home. I dropped the bag with my new dress on the sofa and trudged over to the shower, figuring that I might as well start getting ready. But, just as I switched it on, there was a knock on the door. Wrapped in my towel I hurried over to the door. It could only be my sister.

"Sasha," I greeted with a smile.

She stepped over the threshold to my place without saying a word. She nodded at me, the straps of her handbag held in her teeth as she rooted through her pockets for something. When she was done, she plucked the leather handle from her mouth and gave me a massive grin.

"Hey," she gave me a quick hug, and then zoomed in on the bag I had dumped on the sofa. "Ooh, what's that?"

"I got a dress for going out tonight," I explained, and she opened her mouth, her eyes lighting up, but I held my hand up to stop her before she got too excited. "Eleanor's dragging me out to this male strip thing," I rolled my eyes. "She says it's to help her get over the break-up, but she's just trying to hook up with the lead dancer."

"Oh," Sasha wrinkled her nose up. "Doesn't sound much like your kind of thing."

"It's not." I shook my head at her. "But she's going through a break-up and I want to help her out, you know?"

"And where was she when you split up with…what was his name?" Sasha called over her shoulder as she headed into the kitchen to make herself a cup of tea. She was the only person who could get away with just turning up at my house and treating it like she owned the place.

I followed her into the kitchen. "Yeah, okay, whatever," I said following her into the kitchen and waving my hand at her. I didn't want to think too hard on the fact that she was right. Eleanor hadn't been there for me when I'd split up with my ex, Frank, eighteen months ago. She just didn't deal well with the big dramatic stuff, she'd told me, and she'd been convinced that what I needed was time and space to heal myself. I was sure what I needed was support from my best friend, but I was too gutted to do much more than loll around the flat feeling sorry for myself.

She started to fill the kettle. "Do you want a cup?"

I shook my head.

"Let's get a look at this dress, then." She put the kettle on and herded me back to my small living room. "See if I can bring it in for you."

"Okay, let me get into it." I quickly threw on the dress once more, and spread my hands out and did a twirl. "What do you think?"

I saw the furrow in her brow before she could cover it up. "Hmmm…." She pressed her lips together.

"It's not good, is it?" I muttered, my suspicions confirmed as I plucked at the blue fabric of the dress. It was hard to see if something really suited you in those narrow mirrors shops had in the changing rooms. Now I was sure the dress made me look like a beached whale.

She shook her head and got to her feet, and began to rummage in her handbag.

"What are you looking for?" I asked, walking over to the full length mirror I had in the hallway. God, I looked huge.

"I'm seeing if I have my sewing kit with me," she replied absently, and then I heard her go, "Aha!"

"Do you think you can rescue it?" I asked, shifting back and forth in front of the mirror.

"They don't call me golden fingers for nothing at work."

I glanced at the clock. "I don't have that much time, though. El is coming to pick me up at six thirty."

"You go for your shower." She waved her hand airily. "Leave this thing with me. I'll have it looking fantastic in no time."

"You don't have to-"

"But I want to," she cut me off firmly, the way only she could. She waved her hand again. "Come on, you, out of here."

I did as I was told. I headed straight through to the shower to get myself looking passable for the evening. There were serious upsides to having a sister who worked as a dress-maker, not least the almost magical power she had of turning the worst, most hideous clothes into something really special.

I got out of the shower, blow-dried my hair into soft waves down my back, then I applied mascara and lipstick the best way I knew how. I emerged from the bedroom in my bra and panties and saw Sasha putting the finishing touches on the dress.

"Wow!" I exclaimed, with widened eyes. The dress was practically unrecognizable.

She glanced up at me with an excited grin, the same one she always had on her face when she knew that she had pulled something big off.

"I knew when I was looking at it that there was something special in here somewhere," she blurted out, talking quickly. "The color suits you so much and the cut was good, it just needed a little coaxing. Anyway, try it on. Be careful with the stitching, it's a little delicate."

"Yeah, just what I need, the whole thing coming apart in front of a crowd full of people," I teased, but took the dress gingerly from her and looked down at it. A big grin passed over my face as I looked up at her.

"Thanks for this," I murmured. "It really means a lot to me."

"I'm not letting my little sister go out on the town looking like crap." She got to her feet. "I'm a dressmaker, how would that reflect on me?"

"Fair point," I conceded.

"Now, hurry up and get it on. I'm dying to make that cup of tea I never had."

MADISON

I slipped the dress carefully over my head and Sasha zipped me into it.

It fit like a dream. I could tell that before I even looked at myself. I thought it had fit well enough before, but this was the difference between a dress that could get over my body and a dress that actually enhanced what I had on show.

"How do I look?" I asked.

She smiled. "Go see for yourself."

I walked over to the mirror and my jaw dropped.

She had cut a low neckline into the dress, low enough that I seemed to have magicked up a huge dollop of cleavage from nowhere. She had nipped the dress in around the waist because it made it seem as if I actually had a waist. She had taken up the hemline too. It now came down to just above my knees, and the way it clung to my thighs was borderline scandalous. Well, one thing was for sure, she had effectively made it impossible for me to use this as a work dress. There was no way I was going to be wearing this to any job interviews anytime soon. Unless it was for a very specific type of job.

I twisted back and forth in front of the mirror, taking myself in, and then finally stepped into my only good pair of heels that I owned, black and with a bow that tied around the ankles. Okay, I actually looked pretty good. A smile spread over my face as I looked myself up and down, and I tried to remember why I didn't get dressed up to go out like this more often.

My sister beamed at me. "You look fantastic."

"You think?"

"Absolutely. I don't know why you don't dress like this more often instead of slouching around in those shapeless things you wear." She came over and started fluffing about with the hem. "I knew I could do something with this thing. You really do look amazing, Madison."

I gave her a quick hug. "Thanks for this. I really needed this tonight."

"Yeah, I can imagine," she replied, and I knew immediately she was referring to Eleanor. She had never much liked her, but I tried not to let it get in the way of my relationships with either of them. I told myself Sasha was just protective, but sometimes I wondered if there really was something in Eleanor she needed to protect me from.

Sasha went off to make her tea and I spent a little more time preening myself, making sure my lipstick was perfect and throwing back a bottle of water to make sure that however much I had to drink tonight it wouldn't leave me with too brutal a hangover the next day. A couple of minutes before half six, there was a knock on the door.

"Oh, that'll be Eleanor." I jumped to my feet, and wobbled on my heels and had to catch the arm of the sofa. God, I was just not good at these dangerous things. I could have broken my neck back there.

I buzzed her in, and opened the door to find myself face to face with Eleanor in her full-glamour mode. She looked damn good, in a short, sparkly silver sheath dress that was practically blinding me even in the dim lighting of the hall outside my apartment. Add to the fact that her heels were high and her hair was teased out and huge, it made her virtually impossible to miss, even from miles away. Which would be a good thing, if she intended to catch the eye of the Subway guy.

The only thing that wasn't shining about her was the frown marring her forehead as she cast her gaze over me. I felt my mouth go a little dry as she looked me up and down.

"What's the matter?"

"Your dress," she blurted out.

"Don't you like it?" I struck a pose playfully, but she didn't seem overly amused.

She brushed past me and into the apartment. "Is that the same dress?" she asked, crossing her arms over her chest. There was that furrow in her brow again, letting me know that somehow I'd done something wrong.

"Yeah," I nodded, and pointed to the kitchen where Sasha was still rumbling about. "Sasha did a little work on it for me. I think it looks nice. Don't you like it?"

"It just looks a little…" she trailed off, giving me a long look up and down once more.

Sasha emerged from the kitchen, and her lips tightened when she saw that Eleanor was already there.

"It just looks a little tarty, that's all," she finally finished up, and I felt my cheeks flood with heat at her words.

"I can go change into something else," I suggested, my chin dropping in embarrassment.

"I think you should. Go on then. Quickly."

"No fucking way," Sasha said firmly, shooting some serious daggers in the direction of Eleanor. "You look fantastic, and I worked too hard on that for you not to go out in it now."

"Fine," Eleanor sighed, tossing her hair over one shoulder as though this was the biggest inconvenience she could imagine. "You don't have time to change anyway, the taxi's already waiting outside."

I gave Sasha another quick hug. "See you soon, okay?"

"I'll lock up before I leave," she replied, throwing another venomous glance at Eleanor. "Have a good night."

Her words were barbed even if they seemed innocent, and I knew that they were aimed at Eleanor and not me. I got where she was coming from. Sometimes, I felt as though I wanted someone who called herself my friend to treat me with a little more respect, but I knew that she had been through a lot these last few weeks so I couldn't expect too much from her.

We headed out to the taxi.

MADISON

Eleanor wasn't saying much, eyes fixed on some point out the window, not bothering to even glance over at me. I tugged the hem of my dress down and frowned. Was it because I had gotten all dressed up? Did she think I looked better than her or something? I couldn't help but wonder if she'd been so enthusiastic about that dress because she'd known that it was quite dowdy and would make her appear even more splendid, but now that I'd actually turned the heat up a little she didn't like it one bit. Which kind of surprised me, how could I steal her thunder. She was by far more attractive than me.

We arrived and picked up the tickets that Eleanor had booked on-line. I looked at the price on my ticket and gulped. That could feed me for nearly two weeks. She must have bought the best tickets in the house. We headed towards the entrance doors. The foyer was packed-out with people, the vast majority of them women, and the place was crackling with a tension that I wasn't sure I'd ever felt before in my life.

"Holy shit, this place is packed," I yelled to Eleanor over the sound of the crowd.

She glanced over at me and finally a smile appeared on her face, and I felt a wave of relief hit me, as she seemed to actually be having a good time after all.

"Yeah, well, he's not going to see anyone but me," she replied, pointing up to the enormous billboard that showed off a giant, blown-up picture of Chad Weston. His eyes were lowered to the ground, but his body spoke for itself, and I felt a little flutter in my chest as I took him in. I had never been one for guys who were hot in that really showy, obvious way but he was...hell, he was something else entirely, and I had to admit it was doing it for me.

We were jostled around on our way to the front of the queue, but finally, we made our way into the theatre and took our seats. Even in the dark, the place was bathed with a warm pink lighting that made my heart beat a little faster. It looked like we were heading for the front row. So he could see Eleanor, no doubt, or at least that had to be what was going through her mind.

"Are you sure about this?" I asked Eleanor again, suddenly nervous for what was about to come.

She glanced over at me, brow furrowed with annoyance. "Of course, I am. Come on, sit down, you're in everyone's way."

I took my seat and my heart fluttered when I realized that he would likely be able to see me, too, and I was suddenly glad that Sasha had worked her magic on this dress. I wanted to look good tonight, wanted to look really good, wanted to look better than anyone had seen me before.

It must have been the atmosphere pulsing through the room that had me thinking that way, because I had never felt anything like it before as long as I'd lived. It was like a hen night turned up to twenty, to a thousand times more intense. All these women talking and giggling and occasionally bursting out into little shrieks of excited laughter, as though they could barely keep inside how badly they wanted this. I glanced over at Eleanor, smiling, hoping that she would give me some of that same connection, but she was sitting there staring at the stage with a slight frown on her face. She was probably coming up with a game plan inside her head that didn't include me. I glanced around at the groups of friends laughing and talking and knocking back gulps of their cocktails, and wondered where I had gone wrong that I was missing out on that part of the evening right now.

Suddenly, the house lights lowered, and Eleanor tapped excitedly on my knee, then cupped her hands around her mouth and let out a long whoop, one that blended in with all the rest of the noise coming out of the audience. The excitement in the air was palpable, and I found my heart start beating faster too. I was actually getting into it and couldn't wait to see what this evening had to bring.

"Ladies…" A loud, cheesy voice boomed from the speakers around the venue. "Welcome to…The Man Up Project!"

The rest of what he was saying was drowned out in a series of shrieks of excitement, and I had to grin as the curtain ran up and revealed the men waiting for us behind it. There were at least a dozen of them. I didn't have the time or inclination to count, but they were all moving as though they were in total and utter control of their bodies, totally calm, totally controlled, totally, totally, totally hot. And all of them were stripped to the waist, showing of their insane bodies, sculpted abs and strong arms and bulging pecs.

I scanned the stage to see where the leading man was hiding himself, but I couldn't make him out.

Maybe they saved him for later. It was hard to focus, given the music pulsing out of the speakers and the noise of the crowd. Most of them were on their feet, but Eleanor was still sitting down, as though she hoped that being different might be what attracted the attention of the Subway fame, when he finally arrived, that was.

Still, I wasn't going to sit around having a miserable old time just because she wasn't ready to have fun yet and, taking even myself by surprise, I got to my feet and began swaying my hips back and forth a little to the music. It felt good, really good. There was a whoop from right behind me and I turned around to find the woman in the seat behind ours giving me the thumbs-up. I grinned and flashed her the same sign back. Then I quickly turned my attention back to the stage where the men were dancing, in perfect harmony to the same pulsing beat of the retro dance track that was blasting out over the speakers.

That song came to an end, and the stage was dipped into blackness once more; the audience quieted, as though sensing that something good was about to happen.

At last, when the atmosphere in the room could be cut with a knife: he emerged.

MADISON

There was no need for me to squint to second-guess who he was. Even without getting a proper look at him, I knew this had to be the main man. The lights were so low that I could barely make him out, but he had this presence about him. The way he strode onto that stage through the piles of men in front of him let everyone in that theatre know that he was the one in charge, that it was him they needed to watch out for.

As he stood there on stage, I stared at him, taking him in, unable to tear my eyes away from him. He was fully-dressed but somehow, despite the gorgeous half-naked men around him, he was the only thing in the world that mattered to me and, for a split second, I was sure I saw him looking back at me.

My heart jittered to a stop in my chest as our eyes met.

Then he lowered his gaze once more, just as he did on the poster, and took his position at the center of the stage. The moment was broken, that moment that had passed between us, where I had been sure that there had been that flicker of something real and raw and divine in that look he gave me.

The silence around the room continued for another long moment. Then, as the lights came up, so did the noise. I realized that I had been holding in a breath, and let it out with a long gasp.

His head snapped up and he faced the crowd for the first time, and the women's screams reached crescendo pitch. The atmosphere in the room was incredible, indescribable. Even Eleanor got to her feet. I supposed the sight of him here in real life in front of her was enough to get her to forget any games she might have had and just go for it.

The way he moved was something different to the rest of the guys who had opened the show. Sure, they hit their marks alongside him, just the same way he did, but he oozed a kind of unique confidence and charisma, the kind of thing you couldn't learn with practice. He moved his body like he knew how much everyone in that room wanted him, something that I couldn't relate to. I had always felt a little out-of-place in my own body, and I longed for the kind of confidence that he seemed to own so effortlessly.

Eleanor moved like she was starting the seduction right there and then, and I pressed my lips together and tried not to judge her too harshly for it. She had just been through a break-up, after all, and I shouldn't take whatever she was going through too seriously. Everyone needed some space to relax and blow off some steam. Maybe even me.

After the first song was done, the lights fell low again, the only spotlight was on him. I grinned up at him from where I was standing, and I was sure that he looked down at me once more. I felt myself flush a bright red as soon as his eyes were on me, and embarrassed I glanced away at once. There was just something unbelievably erotic about having him look at me like that.

"Now…" he spoke into his mic. His voice was deep and sexy, and another series of shrieks went up from the audience around me. He seriously owned this place, and he had barely been on-stage for three minutes.

"Put your hand up if you don't want to come up on stage with me tonight," he grinned, casting a look around the audience. I looked around and saw only about a dozen hands in the whole place that went up, from friends who looked as though they'd been dragged here by someone else. I bit my lip and returned my gaze to the stage, and there he was, looking down at me again.

"Because I'm going to need someone to come up here and give me a hand." He looked over the audience once more. Another cheer raised the roof.

"Who's going to help me?"

Pretty much every single woman in that room seemed as though she would have been happy to volunteer, and I whooped right along with them, letting him know that I was very much in their midst. He lifted his finger, letting it rove over the crowd, and then, to my utter shock-

It came to rest on me.

I stood there and just stared at him for a moment. No. Out of all the women in this room, there was no way that he was pointing at me. I glanced over at Eleanor, and I instantly figured out from the foul look she was giving me that yes, he really was pointing at me.

"In the blue dress down there," he announced, smiling directly at me. "Get up here, Gorgeous."

Me gorgeous. Did he just call me gorgeous? I continued to just stand there, peering up at him as though I had no idea what he was asking me. And then, I felt a nudge in my side. The woman next to me, a big smile on her face, was pointing to the stage.

"Go on you lucky thing, get up there!" she ordered me. I forgot about Eleanor glowering beside me. I beamed and grinned and blushed and finally did as I was told. The crowd whooped me along, and I felt as though my feet weren't touching the ground.

I blinked in the bright lights of the stage, feeling like I had been caught out in the light of a million searchlights, but then I felt his arm slip around my waist and everything else in the room dropped away.

MADISON

"And what's your name?" he asked. He looking out on to the crowd and engaging everyone in the room, but, at the same time, I felt as though I was the only thing there that mattered to him. My toes curled in my heels as I inhaled his sweet scent; he was wearing an expensive after-shave, something deep and masculine and musky, and I wanted to bury myself in it and never come out.

"Madison," I replied softly, looking into his eyes. They were so blue and so bright, even more so than they'd seemed from my seat. The way they glinted at me made something light up deep in my stomach.

"Madison," he repeated, and the crowd hollered once more. "Good to meet you, Madison. You ready to help me out?"

"Yeah," I bit my lip, a bit embarrassed, and grinned at him, and I noticed that his thumb was tracing along my waist a little. Did he do this with everyone he brought up on stage?

One of the men he'd been dancing with pulled out a chair from backstage, and placed it down in the spotlight. The light spread and softened as Chad guided me down into the seat, pushing me gently until I was sitting down and staring up at him. He was practically naked in only a pair of underwear, and I could see the shape of his very generous cock even through the fabric. Subway indeed. He leaned in close to my ear, his breath hot on my cheek, and I licked my suddenly dry lips, and tried to keep my cool.

"Just let me know if anything gets too much for you, okay?" he murmured close to my ear, and I knew those words were just for me, and oddly it felt intimate. As we were about to do something sexual and not take part in a performance on stage.

"I will," I promised with a nod, and he drew away and turned back to the crowd, the moment between us dropping away as the music lifted once more.

"Are you ready?" he yelled out to the crowd.

They replied in the affirmative so he turned back to me, and straddled me.

I felt as though my brain had dropped out the back of my head. I gulped as his hard thigh muscles brushed lightly against my body. Then he looked directly into my eyes and I thought I was going to die. Oh, god. This man was something else.

The whole time that he was using me to dance. At first, I felt a little self-conscious, up there on stage, in front of all those people, and being the object of desire for the sexiest man I'd ever me, but then, as he began to use me to move, I forgot all of that and focused entirely on the way he made me feel.

It was impossible not to.

The way he touched me, going slow at first with the beat of the song, pushing a strand of hair back from my face, and leaning in close to my neck, his mouth so warm and so close and so tantalizing, I was finding it hard to keep my head straight.

And then, as the music picked up, he began to really move. He flexed his hips and ground against me, his eyes boring into mine, a slight smile playing at the corner of his sensuous, full lips as though he knew precisely what he was doing to me, and had no intention of letting up. I knew he'd told me that I could stop this whenever I wanted, but no part of me wanted for it to end. No, I wanted more and more.

The song spanned on, but I could barely hear the music any longer, or the screaming of the crowd. In fact, I couldn't concentrate on anything else in the room, but the sound of his breath and mine mingling in the air between us. I could feel my pulse picking up, my body reacting to the way that he was moving on top of me, around me, behind me.

Jesus Christ, I was getting wet!

Standing behind the chair, he slipped his hands down my waist, and hooking his head over my shoulder. I closed my eyes and wondered how obvious it was that I was getting turned on, but I didn't care who saw it. Part of what was getting me off was knowing how sexual he was being with me in front of all these people. I wondered how far he would take it. I wondered how far I would let him…

Because I didn't want to stop. Ever.

The song came to an end, with him right up in my face, only a few inches away from me. He was breathing a little heavily and so was I. I could have sworn I saw his eyes flick down to my mouth for a moment like he was thinking about kissing me right there and then. I tilted my head up, letting him know that I wouldn't have turned it down. He lingered for a moment longer before he seemed to reluctantly pull himself away.

"How about that?" He raised his hands once more and the sound of the crowd began to filter into my brain once more.

I blinked. For a second there when it looked like he was about to kiss me I had forgotten I was up on stage. God, the way he had looked at me. The audience cheered and whooped, and I wondered how many of them were sick with jealousy that I was the one up there and not them. I couldn't see Eleanor's face but I had a feeling she was going to be pretty fucking pissed that he had chosen me and not her.

"How about another one?" Chad asked, and there was another wave of screaming agreement from the audience. He turned to me, with a grin on his face, and shrugged as though he couldn't disappoint his fans. He raised his eyebrows at me, silently asking if this was okay, and I nodded at once. I realized my lips were a little parted, like I had been getting ready for the kiss that had never quite come.

"Wait for me," he said, and ducked backstage for a moment. He returned with something in his hand, and pulled me to my feet. My legs were still so wobbly that I found myself falling against him for support. Thank heavens he was there to prop me up because otherwise I swear, I would have crumpled to the ground in a heap in front of everyone. His body felt so good, so hard and strong next to mine. Without thinking I tentatively laid a hand on his chest. And I didn't even feel slutty.

MADISON

He took a seat in the chair, then guided me in close so I was standing between his legs. I bit my lip and looked down at him. Surely, he didn't expect me to dance for him this time. Or did he? Because I had two left feet and no way was I going to humiliate myself in public.

Thank God, dramatically, and in one strong motion, he pulled me on to his lap. The audience went crazy. I had to catch my breath as I fell on top of him. My arms slipped around his neck. I couldn't quite believe that this was happening to me, but I felt his cock pressing into me through the thin fabric of my dress. Suddenly I was filled with a deep craving to slip my fingers beneath his boxers and just take him in my hand and then...

"You want more?" He was addressing that question to the audience, but it was also a question for me.

I nodded at once. There was no way I could have said no at that point. He could have suggested that the two of us have full sex up on that stage in front of everyone, and I would have gone for it. I just wanted to feel him, to feel every inch of him, to take as much of him as I could in one go.

He lifted his hand and revealed that he was holding a can of whipped cream. Needless to say the crowd went crazy. My eyes widened as he handed it to me.

"You want a taste?" he asked.

It took me a moment to realize what it was he was suggesting. He closed his fingers around mine and guided the can to his broad chest. As I stared at him dumbfounded, he raised his eyebrows at me expectantly. Finally, it sunk in.

I took the can and tentatively drew a line of cream down his chest; my eyes were drawn to the rippling muscles there, to the sheer strength of him. I wondered what he could do to me with that kind of power.

And then, feeling bolder than I'd ever felt in my life, I leaned in and licked the cream off his chest. The crowd was hollering, perhaps imagining themselves in my position, or maybe just entertained by how bold I'd suddenly become.

Underneath the cream, I could taste him.

I had never thought about how a man tasted before this, but I could taste him right there, and something about his taste got me really hot all of a sudden. I had been turned-on before, but this was something else, something more.

I placed my hand on his chest and felt the beat of his heart and realized that it was most probably going that fast for reasons other than the crazy dance routine he'd just performed. I looked up at him, my tongue still trailing over his chest, and widened my eyes at him playfully. His hand came to the back of my head as he looked down at me. If he had guided my head downwards I would have gone with it. No complaints and no problems at all.

Once I had taken care of that thin line of cream, I went to put another over his stomach, a little lower down, hungry for him now and uninterested in holding back my desires. I bit my lip as I drew the line down, closer to his underwear than before, and I might have been crazy, but I was sure I could see his cock stirring to life beneath the fabric. I wanted to touch him down there so badly, but I also didn't want to do anything that might get in the way of me being up here. I had no idea what the rules were, but I had a feeling that straight-up getting down on my knees and licking his dick would probably be a little too far.

The neckline of my dress had inched down a little, and I noticed his eyes straying down to my cleavage. Oh, he could have those babies any time he wanted. I leaned down, and let my tongue trail along that spot below his belly button, that sensitive part that made his chest jerk up suddenly. The crowd was screaming their encouragement, and I loved how in-control I was right then. He had been the one in charge at first, but he hadn't counted on me being the one to go this far. It had been a long time since I had actually felt this kind of desire and there was no way in hell I was going to pass up the chance to act on it now that I had been given the opportunity.

He stroked a strand of hair away from my face as I licked and kissed the sweetened cream from his body. I found myself running my hands across his arm, letting him know that I felt it too. But was this all an act? Did he make every woman he was with feel this good, this wanted, this desired? Did his cock stir at any woman or was it only for me?

Once I was done, he pulled me back on to his lap, shooting a look backstage where I could see a few of the other dancers raising their eyebrows at him expectantly. Reluctantly, Chad got to his feet. He took a deep breath before he turned to the audience once more, like he was forcing himself back into the mindset to perform all over again.

Women roared their approval as he approached the front of the stage once more, guiding me along with him, his arm still tucked around me tight as though he didn't want to let me go.

"Give it up for Madison!" he called out, and there was a huge round of applause.

I leaned against him, not wanting this to be over. I knew there had to be more to the show that just turning me on, but I didn't want there to be.

He leaned down and scooped me up off the ground, making me squeal with surprise. Instinctively, I wound my arms around his neck and clung on tight, for dear life. He made his way off the stage and back down towards my seat. People moved out of the way quickly to let him through.

I let my head rest on his strong shoulder, inhaling his scent one last time, wanting to commit as much of this to memory as I could. I wondered how obvious I was being, and swiftly decided that I didn't give a shit. If I was the kind of person who got up on stage at a male strip show, then I was the kind of person who didn't care what people thought of me when I did.

He placed me back down in front of my seat, and I was sure that was it. It had just been a seriously good play on his part, a practiced performance. A testament to how good he was at his job. But, to my surprise, he produced a small scrap of paper from somewhere I didn't want to think about and tucked it into my cleavage. His fingers just brushing across my breasts. It was enough to send shivers up my spine. He leaned in close, one last time, his mouth brushing for the briefest moment against my ear.

"Call me," he murmured.

MADISON

With my jaw on the floor, I watch him head back on stage to join the rest of the dancers who had come out to pick up where they'd left off. I pulled the note from my chest and saw a series of numbers on it. Was this real? Was this part of the act? It felt real. He couldn't fake that kind of chemistry. Could he?

I turned to Eleanor, and as soon as I saw her face, I knew I was in trouble. Big trouble. She was seething, so much so that I was surprised steam wasn't pouring out of her ears.

"Come on," she grabbed hold of my wrist and pulled me to my feet. "We need to go to the bathroom."

I followed her, stumbling along behind her as she strode out of the theatre. I looked up at Chad and saw him watching us. Defiantly, I flashed him another dizzy smile. As soon as Eleanor and I made it into the bathrooms she turned on me at once, face dark.

"What the fuck was that about?" she snarled, waving her hand in the direction of the stage.

"What do you mean?" I grinned, the paper still clutched tight in my hands.

"You behaved like a bitch out there."

I gasp. "It was just a bit of fun. He picked me, that's all."

"What kind of friend are you? You know that I came here to get with him and you go and take him for yourself," she fumed, raising her eyebrows as though that was supposed to mean something to me.

"I didn't take him," I protested. "And I can't help that he picked me out of the crowd-"

"You could have sent me up instead. You knew I needed this. You didn't even want to come," she pointed out.

I frowned. "I'm sorry, I guess I wasn't thinking in that moment," I apologized, even though I really felt I had nothing to apologize for. But I knew Eleanor, and I knew that if I didn't concede my position to her the rest of the night was going to be a fucking nightmare.

"Yeah, I bet you weren't," she snapped. "Just like you weren't thinking when you put on that dress."

"What do you mean by that?" I ran my hands over my body. I liked the way the dress looked, doubly so now that it had gotten Chad's attention.

"You look cheap," she spat. To my horror, she suddenly plucked the piece of paper from between my fingers.

"Give it back to me," I said, as she crumpled the scrap of paper in her hands. I fought to keep the dismay from my face. It's not that I was expecting to start a relationship with

Chad or anything, but I had wanted to at least see, to check if it had been his real number, and if he had actually wanted me.

"All he wants from you is a one night stand." She looked me up and down, her voice echoing cruelly through the room. It felt as if it was filling up my head making me feel quite sick. "I mean, look at you. That's what you're dressed for, isn't it?"

"El," I protested, using the pet name that she had tried to stop me from calling her a few years before. "Please, come on, it was just a bit of fun—"

"Yeah, well, I was pretty sure I was the one who was meant to be having the fun." She cocked her head at me, and then, before I could stop her, she ducked into one of the stalls, dropped the piece of paper into the toilet bowl, and flushed.

"No, Ellie, why would you do that?" I gasped as I watched my only chance at seeing Chad again spiral away into the toilet bowl.

"Because this was meant to be about me," she snapped. She walked to the door. "And I'm not going to forget that. I'm going to find him now. So you just enjoy the rest of your night."

She stormed out of the bathroom and left me standing there all alone, staring after her, wondering what in the hell had just happened and how responsible I actually was for it. I had never seen her that angry before in my life, or so I thought. And then it hit me.

All the times that she had spoken to me like this seemed to rush up and overwhelm me all at once. There was a reason my sister hated her so much. Because this was her game, the way she'd always treated me. I always had to be less-than her, always had to be propping up her pathetic ego. And now, as the sound of the flushing toilet faded away, she had just blown my chances for a bit of fun with a hot guy because she couldn't handle the fact that he had picked me over her.

I retreated into one of the stalls and closed the door behind me. I wasn't sure how long I was in there, trying to make sense of what had just hit me like a ton of bricks. Women came into the toilets, they laughed, they talking among themselves, they used the other stalls. They even tried my door. Then they left.

I felt stupid for not guessing it sooner, but now, here I was, stuck on a night I had never wanted to come out on in the first place, and wondering why the hell I had let that kind of woman stay in my life for so long.

Eventually, the music and the cheers and the chatter faded away outside the bathroom, and I got to my feet and went out. I washed my hands and automatically checked my make-up.

She would probably already be out of here, and knowing her probably with Chad.? Would he fall for her game? My heart sank at the thought, and I pushed it out of my head as I made my way out of the bathroom. I tried not to cringe at how much the taxi was going to cost back to my place now that I wasn't splitting it with anyone.

My feet were killing me. Peeling my heels off my feet, I trudged out on the bathroom, and out into the lobby. The place was empty. Everyone else had headed home, likely at the end of a good night with their friends. I could still remember how it had felt to arrive here, how it had felt to be surrounded by the buzz of excitement that hung in the air as we waited for the show to begin. That felt like so long ago now.

"Hey," called a voice from behind me.

MADISON

I turned around tiredly, thinking it would be an usher letting me know that the place was closed and telling me to go home already. But, to my utter shock, I found myself looking at the man who had caused all the commotion in the first place.

"Oh!" I squeaked, blinking at him stupidly.

"Sorry, did I sneak up on you?" He grinned. He was fully-dressed now, in a pair of dark jeans and a form-fitting black shirt that didn't do justice to the muscles underneath that I had so recently had a front row seat to.

"Yeah, a little," I admitted. "But it's okay."

"Are you alright?" he asked, frowning.

I shook my head and lowered my gaze. I felt embarrassed that I was dragging him into this, but I knew it was written all over my face. I really was upset about everything that had happened over the course of the evening. Well, not what had gone down with him, but all that had happened with Eleanor still felt like a damn kick to my teeth.

"What happened?" He moved towards me, and placed a comforting hand on my arm. I felt that explosion of tingles once more, as soon as our bodies connected, but he was just being nice, that was it.

"My friend and I had a falling out and she left without me." I shrugged, trying to sound as though I didn't give a shit, but my voice shook. I just cared too much about everything. That was what had gotten me into this mess in the first place. If I had just been able to turn Eleanor down for this evening none of this would have happened.

"Man, that sucks." He cocked his head at me, and I looked up into those bright eyes and reminded myself that this hadn't been a complete write-off, after all. As long as I live I will never forgot what happened on stage. That one hot gorgeous man wanted by a theater full of women picked me, wanted me.

"Can I buy you a drink?" he suggested. "The bar's still open. Seems like you could use it."

"Seriously?" I raised my eyebrows at him. He must have taken my shock at him actually asking me out for a dink as some kind of reluctance, because he held his hands up at once.

"Hey, if I'm overstepping—"

"No, no, I'd love to," I assured him, and to my astonishment I found myself fluttering my eyelashes at him even though I was still cut up about everything that had just gone down with Eleanor. But somehow, that hurt seemed to drop away when I looked into his sparkling blue eyes.

A smile cracked over his face, and he held his hand out to me. "Come on, babe. I'm going to show you a good time."

CHAD

I had never had it happen like that before, not in my life.

I had used so many women from the audiences of my shows before, so many women who anyone else might have thought of as hot, sexy, or desirable. And sure, I enjoyed the attention for as long as it lasted, but I never wanted anything more from them. But this woman?

This woman was a whole other story.

I watched her as she was dragged unceremonious by her jealous friend towards the bathroom. I knew she was about to get her ear chewed off, but all I could see was the way that dress clung to her. It was enough to get me hard again.

I had noticed her the moment I stepped out onstage, the rest of the crowd vanishing from my line of vision as my surprised eyes took her in. In that blue dress, with that cleavage, the way her hair tumbled down around her shoulders like it was waiting for me to run my hands through it.

No wonder her friend had been jealous.

The bar was quiet, much to my relief. Sometimes the women who'd attended my shows would hang around after it was done in the hopes of catching me. A lot of them threw themselves at me. It was part of the job, I got it, but sometimes it was a little exhausting to always have to be on.

But the way Madison looked at me, I knew that she felt that frisson too. She had felt the same connection that had rumbled deep inside me from the second I laid eyes on her. There was no way she could have missed it. From the moment I saw her I wanted her. Even from across the table I could still smell her perfume, something sweet and light and floral, and all I wanted was to bury my face in her neck and lose myself there for a while.

"Hey," she picked up the glass of wine she'd ordered. "So…"

"So," I grinned. I felt like the whole night was spread out in front of us, and there was so much I wanted to do with her, to her.

"Just so you know," she lowered her gaze as though she couldn't believe she was saying this. "I totally would have called you if Eleanor hadn't gotten rid of your number."

"Well, I'm only in town for one night." I shrugged. "You've gotta take those chances, right?"

"Right," she agreed, and I noticed her gaze flicker down to my mouth for a moment. I grinned. I was used to having women attracted to me, but it had been a while since I had felt that attraction burning straight back at them.

"So, what do you do in a town you're only in for one night?" she asked, cocking her head at me, and taking another sip of her wine.

"I don't know." I shrugged again. "Usually I just have a drink and get some rest. Being up there all night is pretty exhausting."

She nodded. "Oh, yeah, I can imagine. I saw the way you were moving up there. It was…uh, pretty intense." She lowered her gaze once more, as though she couldn't believe she was actually talking with me. I saw her force herself to look back up and into my eyes.

"You know I wasn't even going to come to this thing tonight?" she admitted, leaning a little closer.

I leaned in to meet her and caught the sweet scent of her perfume once more. "Oh yeah?" I grinned.

"Yeah, if it hadn't have been for my friend, or rather ex-friend, I wouldn't have met you." She bit her lip. She kept doing that, as though she was trying to keep from blurting out something she didn't intend to. I knew exactly how she felt.

"Well, I guess we have something to thank her for," I remarked, letting my hand stray onto her thigh. She inhaled sharply when I touched her. The warmth of her skin, even through the fabric of her dress, had my cock stirring in my pants once more. I could still remember the way her tongue had felt on my skin, the warmth of her breath. Fuck, it was incredible, but I wanted to just grab her by the hips and fuck her right there on stage.

Slowly, she lifted her gaze to meet mine. I had seen desire enough times to know it, and I could see it in her eyes now what was no doubt reflected in mine. I had to do something. I was in this country for twelve more hours and I was sure as hell going to make the most of my time by spending all of it with her.

I leaned in, breathing deeply, filling my head with the scent of her, and she closed her eyes.

"Chad…" she murmured my name. I could see this tiny drop of wine on the edge of her mouth, and I finally touched my lips to hers and tasted her at last.

Her body trembled as I ran my hand up her leg and let it come to rest on her waist. I wondered how deep her desire went, if she was just testing herself to see how far she could go, or if this was really going to happen. I pulled back, and she leaned her head against mine for a moment, eyes still closed, and flicked her tongue across her full bottom lip.

"Where are you staying?" she asked, her eyes open again.

I realized I had sunk my fingers into her waist, like I was trying to leave an imprint on her. "In the rooms upstairs." I flicked my eyes upwards. I could feel the gaze of the bartender on me, the few other patrons in this bar sense the chemistry between us. I didn't care.

"Take me there," she demanded, her lips parting slightly.

CHAD

I needed no more encouragement. It took everything I had not to scoop her up, flip her over my shoulder, and carry her luscious curves up there like the caveman I felt like right now, but patience won the day.

She tossed back the last of her wine and I held out my hand to her. She slipped her hand into mine, glancing around at everyone we were leaving behind, and letting out this adorable little giggle that made me want to bite her lip.

We made our way up a set of stairs to the rooms that the theatre left open for the performers to take advantage of. Mine wasn't much, but it was plenty enough for us for the rest of the night. I pulled my key out of my pocket as we turned onto the carpeted corridor that led to the bed where I thought I'd be sleeping alone tonight. She squeezed my hand and fuck, there is no way to stop myself.

I swung her around, pushed her up against the door in one motion, running my hand up her thigh, over her waist, and letting it come to a stop on her face. Her breath was fast, those gorgeous tits rising and falling so quickly it was hard not to stare, but instead, I lifted my gaze to meet hers, and kissed her once more.

This time there was no messing around, no holding back, no having to remind myself over and over again that there was not just an audience watching us but my friends and manager, who would likely be shocked. Now, it was just us, our bodies pressed together as I parted her lips with my tongue and kissed her properly.

She let out the softest little moan, somewhere between satisfaction and frustration for more, as I kissed her and I realized that I was already getting hard just touching her like this. How could one person turn me on this much?

All those women out there, all of them screaming and cheering and throwing themselves at me, and not one of them had done anything for me. Yes, she could effortlessly turn me into a raging bull. She moved her hips slightly, on instinct more than anything else, and I pushed my tongue roughly into her mouth and gripped her hair in my balled fist.

I was going to make damn sure that she never forgot me.

"Take me inside," she breathed, running one hand tentatively over my back and drawing me in close. I didn't need told again. I unlocked the door and the two of us tumbled into the room, practically falling over each other in our desperation to finally do this. I could still remember the weight of her in my lap as she tantalizingly and knowingly pressed herself against my cock while she played the innocent volunteer.

I intended to make her pay for that ten times over.

I picked her up, winding my arms around her and kissing her hard as I walked back towards the dresser. I dropped her down on top of it. She hooked her ankles around me. Only the thin fabric of her panties was between me and having all of her. It hit me that I could have just reached down and ripped them off and fucked her raw right there and then, but I had other plans, other things I wanted to get to first.

I kissed down her neck, slowing my pace a little. She let her hand rest on my chest, feeling my heartbeat. The sweetness of her skin was everything I'd thought it would be. Her mouth had tasted of a rich, deep wine, but her neck was all her, delicate and feminine. I grazed my teeth over her throat before I moved up to nuzzle at that spot where her neck met her ears. It made her squirm frantically and drew another one of those desperate little moans from her mouth. I decided right then and there that it was going to be my goal to get her to make as much noise as I possibly could. I didn't care if she made more noise than that entire audience out there had tonight. I wanted to hear her scream. I wanted to know she was as lost to me as I already found myself lost to her.

Truth was I was drunk on her. There was this mix deep within her this blend of something good and something bad, and I couldn't wait to tap into it and see what happened when I set it loose. Or when she did.

"Mmm, you taste so fucking good," I breathed, and she shivered once more, her eyes wide as I returned to her face to kiss her again. I held her there, just for a moment, almost tender as I trailed my tongue over her bottom lip before I drew it into my mouth and bit down softly. She moaned and ran her hands over my arms, my shoulders, my chest.

I bit her again, but harder, and earned a groan of pleasure for my troubles.

I started to work my way down once more, this time not stopping at her neck. I pushed the straps of her dress down over her shoulders and off her arms. She crossed her hands, as if on instinct, over her chest, like she wasn't used to letting people look at her like this. I liked that. I kissed her again, slowly pulling her arms aside.

"You don't have to hide from me," I whispered. "You're beautiful."

Slowly, she let her arms drop down by her sides. Finally, I got a chance to look at her incredible body full-on; her tits were gorgeous, as heavy and full as ripe fruit, her nipples brown and tempting. I leaned down to take one in my mouth, flickering my tongue against it, and then I pushed the other and sucked them both into my mouth. I sucked and bite them until they were both swollen between my lips. She raked her fingers through my hair and moaned helplessly.

When they were impossible swollen and her moans had become whimpers, I continued on my journey downward, kissing the soft flesh of her stomach, letting my tongue trail low on her belly just the way she had done to me.

She let out a giggle, as though the same thought had occurred to her. I kept going lower and lower until I was on my knees between her legs. I looked up, and found her lips parted, breath coming quickly. I grinned. It was so hot to know she was as turned-on by this as I was.

I took her right leg in my hand and began to kiss it, starting at the ankle. I pulled off her shoe, then moved up the inside of her calf, letting my mouth linger here and there, listening to her reactions. The speed of her breathing picked up pace as I moved closer and closer to her sweet pussy. I paused at the inside of her thigh, finding that sensitive spot that made her whole body tremble with anticipation, and slowly pushing her legs apart I rolled up the hem of her dress.

CHAD

I leaned back to look at her then, at this woman before me. I had known that from the first moment that I had laid eyes on her in that crowd that I had to taste her. I needed her pussy in my mouth, but there was no rush, and I loved nothing more than the thought of getting her to beg me for what I was already so eager to give.

She was wearing a pair of polka dot panties, somehow so innocent, and so filthy at the same time. I moved forward slowly to plant a kiss on her flesh through the fabric. She gasped, then let out a squeak when I moved on and starting kiss down the other side of her leg.

"Please," she begged.

My cock ached at her words. She had seemed nervous at the bar, but I guessed she was as intoxicated on whatever it was that was between us as I was.

"Please?" I prompted, wanting to hear more. I wanted her to tell me every single thing she wanted me to do to her tonight, because there wasn't much that I wouldn't have done to earn those little animal-like noises of pleasure that I was already addicted to.

"Don't … I mean please, do what you were just doing," she whispered, as I reached her calf and pulled off her other shoe.

"What do you mean?" I grinned at her, letting her know that I would need to hear the words come out of her mouth before I would do it.

"You know," she bit her lip.

I hooked my fingers around her panties and held them there, demanding more from her. "Tell me," I ordered her. "I want to hear you say it."

She looked down at me for a moment longer, pressing her lips together, as though no-one had ever asked her for anything so scandalous in her entire life. Is the whole world crazy? How could they not?

"I want you to…" She took a deep breath. "I want you to go down on me."

"Good girl." I nodded approvingly, and pulled her panties off her feet and tossed them aside. I pushed what was left of her dress up and over her hips, grabbed her, and pulled her towards me in one rough motion. She raked her fingers through my hair, audibly excited, belly rising and falling quickly as I pressed my mouth against her pussy for the very first time.

The noise she made was unlike anything I'd ever heard in my life, like something had shattered inside of her for good. I quickly sealed my lips around her clit, flicking my tongue against her a few times before I settled in to a long, slow, lazy pace that told her I was going to make the most of my time right here between her thighs.

I slid my hands under her ass and guided her onto my mouth, wanting to bury myself in there and never come out if I could get away with it. She tasted so sweet, like nectar, that muskiness carving a place out for itself in my memory forever. I made sure to take my time, pulling back and licking up and down her dripping slit, looking up and watching her as I did so. She responded to every little move I made with my tongue like it was an electric shock, her face contorting and creasing with every new move I tried on her.

Sometimes, with the women I'd been with before, they had this habit of trying to look all pulled-together and sexy when I was eating them out, but she had completely given herself over to the pleasure and I couldn't think of anything hotter in the world than that.

My cock was straining against my jeans as I went down on her, stroking her clit over and over again and sinking my fingers into her thick ass as I did so. She groaned loudly, the sound ringing out around the small room, and I knew she was getting close.

I centered in on her clit once more, sucking softly, moving my tongue in gentle motions up and down, up and down, and soon she began to move with me. Holding my head in place, she rocked her hips back and forth. Holding her breath, tensing her muscles, curling her toes, and then finally, finally, coming so hard against my tongue I thought her entire body was going to fall apart.

"Fuck!" she screamed.

Tipping her head back she caught my head in an iron grip with her thighs. Her clit was pulsing on my tongue, and her pussy was slick with my saliva and her juices as she found her climax. For a long, long time the waves came as she jerked against my mouth.

Then, slowly, she came back to find I was still sucking her engorged clit. She pushed my head away roughly, her cunt was too sensitized for any more at that moment. I would have happily spent the rest of the evening turning her into a quivering, coming wreck again and again, but as she leaned down to kiss me my cock was digging into my flesh. It was desperate for release as well.

"That was incredible," she panted, her face looked as though she had just returned from an intergalactic flight. "I've never … Thank you … I …"

"Anytime," I said, and kissed her again. I loved the way the taste of her mingled on our tongues. She slid her hand down my body and gripped my cock, suddenly bold. I growled into her mouth as soon as I felt her fingers up against my erection.

"Fuck me," she murmured into my mouth, and at that moment I knew I just had to have her. There was no question in my mind. I couldn't wait any longer. I wanted to play this game all night long but for now all I needed was to feel that slick, tight pussy wrapped around my massive cock. I just hoped she would be able to take all of me, or I'd have the time to break her in. Spoil her for any other man.

I pulled her from the dresser and turned her around. She whipped off her dress and shot a look at me over her shoulder, a confident smile flickering on her face as she watched me strip down. I wanted to feel my flesh against hers, every part of her, and I needed it now.

I had some condoms in my bag. I reached over to grab one. Tearing the packet open I swiftly sheathed myself.

"Oh, God. You really are Subway Chad, aren't you?" she whispered.

"And you're going to take every last inch inside you."

CHAD

There was a mirror opposite us, and I could see her eyes shining even in the darkness of that room. I grabbed her hip and pulled her closer, and she arched her back to press herself against me.

"I want to feel you inside me. All of you. Every last inch," she breathed, closing her eyes as if she couldn't quite believe it was her saying those words. I wondered if she'd ever done anything like this before. I certainly had, but it had never felt anything close to this. I pressed myself against her slit and sinking my fingers into her hips, and pushed my way inside her for the first time.

"Oh..." she moaned, her head dropping and her fingers tightening their grasp on the counter below her as I entered her for the first time. There weren't words to describe how good she felt around my cock; warm, tight, sweet and all kinds of perfect.

"Oh, you're so big," she breathed.

"Just a bit more," I said, as I pushed another inch into her.

"Is there a lot of more?" she asked, turning to look at me.

"Just a few inches more," I said, and thrust.

"Oh, Chad," she gasped, as I buried myself all the way in.

I held still, and didn't move for a moment as I watched the two of us together in the mirror. My entire cock was buried inside her. Not many women can take all of me. I knew that image would be seared into my memory until the day I died.

"Feel good?" I asked her.

"It's feel amazing. I'm so stretched. So full. It's amazing," she gasps.

That was my signal. I began to move. I didn't hold back. I didn't have it in me to, not after all that I'd had to repress when she had been up on stage with me. She arched her back and pushed herself back against me, moving hard, her eyes open, but half-glazed as though she could barely believe that this was happening for real. I ran my hand up her bare back and wrapped her hair around my fist, tugging it back, watching the spasm of pain and pleasure that passed over her face at my rough handling.

I had to slow down, not wanting to come too quickly, but I knew I wouldn't last forever. Seeing her like this, bent over in front of me, her thick ass shuddering with every thrust into her swollen pussy, it was enough to get my balls tingling. I was so close.

I slammed deep into her and didn't move for a moment. She moaned when I slipped my hand between her legs to find her clit once more. She turned her head and stared at me in the mirror, and the look on her face told me she was desperate for more. It sent a new rush of desire through my system that almost made me feel drunk for her.

"Come for me," I growled. "Come for me, Madison, I want to feel you come…"

I didn't have the brain space to articulate what I wanted from her any more than that, but luckily for me, it seemed to be enough for her. Her thighs trembled, her lips parted, and her body seemed to slacken beneath mine as her pussy pulsed around my cock, milking me, squeezing the last drops of pleasure from my cock.

A deep groan seemed to come from far down inside her, escaping her lips as this strange strangled cry was torn out of her she climaxed once more. Seeing the look on her face, feeling her body give out around me once more was all I needed to push me over the edge.

"Fuck," I grunted, as I felt myself go over the edge. The pleasure seemed to rip through me, setting me alight, every limb turning to ash as I did my best to keep myself upright. The sensations exploded through every nerve ending in my body. I held myself inside her for a long while, before I came back down to Earth, before I slowly pulled out.

She was still gasping for air from her own intense orgasm. I looped my arm around her waist and pulled her up and onto the bed, where she let her head sink gratefully back into the pillows.

"Holy fuck," she mouthed, the words so quiet I could hardly make them out. "That was…"

"Was?" I cocked an eyebrow and slid down the bed next to her. I could already feel something building in me again, at the sight of her generously curvy body splayed out on the sheets for me like this.

"What do you mean?" she asked, suddenly flushing a little as though she was embarrassed by what we had just done. The color on her cheeks was so cute that I had to lean forward and plant a kiss on each one. She squirmed as I let my hand trace over her stomach and down between her legs once more. Oh, this night was so far from over.

MADISON

When I woke the next morning to the thin light filtering through the window opposite the bed, it took me a moment to work out where the hell I was. And then, as he stirred next to me and turned over, the night before came back.

Even though I hadn't had more than a glass or two of wine, I felt as though most of the night was still a blur for me. It had all been...hell, it had been more than I had ever dreamed could happen to me.

The whole night had been...it had been something plucked straight out of a fantasy that I would have written off as impossible for someone like me. But, as I carefully turned I saw the man in bed next to me, and it all came flooding back. All of it. In toe curling flashes.

It had all happened.

I had come so many times that I had lost track of the what and the how and where he had fucked me. It had started on the counter, when he had buried his face between my legs and made me come with his tongue. Then he had flipped me around to take me from behind. And then, just when I thought we were done and he was going to boot me out, he laid me down in this bed and climbed on top of me once more and…mmm. Yeah. All of that stuff had happened. Him on top, me on top, me blowing him, him eating me out, making me come with his fingers, his cock, his mouth…

Never, ever in my entire life, had there been anything like the way this played out. The chemistry between us was something I had never imagined actually existed before he had pushed me up against the door and kissed me last night. Before I had tasted his tongue in my mouth I would never have believed this kind of passion was real.

I had assumed that my attraction to him sprang from the fact that I couldn't have him, and that he was just blowing off some steam with some chick he thought was cute, but this was something else entirely. It crackled in the air the whole night long as our hands hungrily explored every part of our bodies until we were both beyond exhausted and fell asleep in each other's arms.

But now that I was awake, in the bright light on the day after, and in this hotel room with a man I barely knew, I couldn't help but feel more than a little embarrassed. I had never done anything like this for a reason, and that was because I had no clue how to handle the morning after.

I looked at my dress, my underwear, my shoes, all strewn around the room, and my heart sank when I realized that I was going to have to walk home in them. Everyone would know that I'd stayed out all night.

Damn, but I couldn't stay here; he was going back to America, and I wasn't going to hang about and make a fool of myself pretending that there was a hope in hell he might stick around a little longer for someone like me.

I snuck around the room, gathering myself, and wondered if the doors downstairs were even open yet. Maybe I'd have to hang around until someone came and opened them up for me. How mortifying…

"Hey."

A voice from the bed caught me off-guard, and I turned to find Chad smiling sleepily at me. His hair was a mess but his body was as flawless as ever, even more so now that I could actually see it in the light of the sun filtering in.

I chewed on my bottom lip. He has suck on it so much last night it was feeling a little raw, but I didn't care. I would permanently be biting my lip while he was around just to keep from groaning at how damn hot he always looked. Those sculpted abs, that taut chest, his strong arms…

"Where do you think you're going?" He climbed out of bed, stood, and stretched. Oh my! I bit my lip again. Yes, he was stark naked and his enormous cock was already stirring to life, despite the fact that we couldn't have been asleep more than a few hours.

"I was headed home." I gestured towards the door, lowering my gaze, suddenly more than a little embarrassed for him to be seeing me like this. In the harsh light of day, no doubt, he would be wondering why the hell he had taken me to bed when he could have had any one of the stunning women who had been at his show the night before.

"Really?" He cocked an eyebrow, came towards me, wrapped

his powerful arms around me, and buried his face in my neck. "You got somewhere else to be, baby?"

"No," I admitted, closing my eyes and savoring the feel of him so close to me one last time. It stung, knowing that I would have to leave him soon, but I knew it would have been stupid of me to stay.

"Then why the big rush?" he asked, pressing his mouth against my shoulder and grinding against me. I could feel myself getting aroused again, and those thoughts of insecurity and worry slid out of my head like so much wet paint.

"I don't want to hold you up," I said. "You have to go back soon…"

"Not that soon," he replied, slipping his hand down and letting it rest on my lower belly. He skimmed his fingers over my bush and I felt another jolt of desire lance through me. And there I was thinking I'd tapped out my reserves of pure lust after all we did the night before. But it was still there, that chemistry, as rich and intense as it had been the night before.

That didn't happen often.

"Yeah, but I don't want to be waiting around for you to go," I admitted softly. It was true. When he went, I had to go back to my life, to the reality of no job and a best friend who treated me like shit, but who would probably try to find some way to slide back into my life when this was all over.

"Then don't," he suggested. "Come back with me."

"What?" I stared at him in shock.

"Come with me," he repeated.

"Yeah, right," I said with a grin, as if I appreciated his joke. I would have loved to go back with him, but there was no way in hell he would pick up some woman he'd spent one night with and whisk her all the way back across the world with him.

"I'm not kidding," he replied, and I turned to face him. I was surprised at how unselfconscious I felt, even exposed in the light like this with him. Normally I would be doing everything I could to cover myself up, but he kept his hand on my waist and held me in close.

"What the hell are you talking about?" I demanded, brushing my nose against his softly and closing my eyes, letting myself get lost in this fantasy of him for a few more moments yet.

"I mean, come back with me to America." He pulled back and looked me dead in the eyes. There wasn't a hint of mockery in them. "I'll pay. Just for a while…until we figure this thing between us out."

"I…" I stared at him for a long moment. I had no job to go back to, my best friend had proved herself to be a completely selfish bitch, and this gorgeous man with whom I'd shared the craziest night of my life had just invited me to travel across the world with him, on his dollar.

I blinked at him. No. I couldn't. I didn't know him from Adam. Could I?

I had told myself that I couldn't do this. That I couldn't go to this show, or stand up to Eleanor, or get up on stage with him, or touch him, or make love to him, but I had done all of that. And it had brought me here. Why the hell should I stop now? With a rush of nerves and excitement, I nodded.

"I'll do it," I agreed, a smile half-a-mile wide spreading over my face.

"Seriously?" His face lit up. "You'll come back with me?"

"Just for a while," I warned. "Just to see how it goes-"

"Obviously," he scooped me off my feet and laid me down on the bed, and slid on top of me. Instantly, my heart-rate went through the roof. Nuzzling into my neck, he continued. "Just for a while or," he repeated my words back to me.

Then began to kiss down my chest and over my stomach, and before I knew it, I was completely lost to this man once more. I wasn't sure whether I had just made an amazing decision or a bat-shit crazy one, but in the throes of ecstasy, as if from far away I heard his voice say, "Just for a while, or until you get it, that you are mine. All mine. Forever."

The End
or
Maybe NOT!
Watch out for the next installment in their story.

ABOUT THE AUTHOR

If you want me I'll be waiting for you here...

Made in the USA
Columbia, SC
26 January 2019